Hiding Behind The Couch Series

Breaking Waves

by
Debbie McGowan

Beaten Track
www.beatentrackpublishing.com

Contents

Prologue 1

To Have 7

To Hold 17

In Sickness… 45

For Better, For Worse 57

From This Day 65

About the Author 77

By the Author 78

Beaten Track Publishing 82

Prologue

A MIDSUMMER'S EVENING, WITH the solstice nearing; it was late yet still daylight, the sun at the perfect height to bedazzle as it slowly set, always to their right. This was the final leg of their journey, and what a journey it had been. For it began, not at their departure from their wedding reception, nor at the point where they exchanged their vows, but thirty years before, in a primary school classroom...

"This is George," Mrs. Kinkade announced to the class, her hands resting on the shoulders of the child standing in front of her. "Now, George, as you can see, there are lots of free chairs. Where would you like to sit?"

George looked around, bewildered, and pointed at the square formed by two tables to his left.

"Excellent. Off you go, then. Joshua will show you where to find everything, won't you, Joshua."

Josh kept his out-of-focus gaze on the blur of green fields and sheep, wriggling his fingers to re-establish the physical connection.

George squeezed his hand. "What are you thinking about?"

"Nothing much." Josh turned and met his new husband's quizzical expression with a smile so bright it almost outshone the halo of sunlight surrounding him. "The new boy," he said. George lowered his eyes; Josh laughed at his bashfulness. "You still haven't told me why you chose my table."

George's memory of that very first day in his new school still caused a riot of emotion he couldn't fully articulate. It had all seemed to happen at once—his dad leaving, moving house, changing school—huge, life-changing events, completely beyond his control. But then, what eight-year-old held the reins to their own destiny? The decisions were for adults to make, and he, little Georgie Morley, went along with whatever was required of him—until that very first day in his new school, faced with his very first decision.

Where would you like to sit?

"You were closest," he said.

"Fibber. Shaunna and Adele were sitting right in front of you."

George lifted Josh's hand and pressed it to his chest. "Closest to here."

Josh gave a small, involuntary gasp that sent a shiver chasing right through him.

"Are you cold?" George wrapped his arms around Josh to maximise body contact.

"I'm going with *yes*," Josh said with a grin.

George laughed. "Do you want my jacket? I can probably reach—"

"No." Josh shuffled closer. The shivering diminished and he sighed in contentment.

George planted a kiss on Josh's head, keeping his lips and nose nestled in his hair, breathing in the sweet, familiar scent. Coconut, sandalwood, citrus and coffee—the blend that was uniquely Josh and had been so since they were teenagers. Sometimes, when he was at university, George would catch a whiff of someone who maybe wore the same cologne or used the same shampoo. If mixed with the smell of coffee, it would remind him of how much he was missing Josh. Not that he'd ever stopped missing him, and their uni days were of the time before mobile phones could be found in every student's pocket, but whenever he had enough money, George would call from the payphone in the halls of residence, just to hear Josh's voice.

"*Hi.*"

"*Hi, yourself.*"

"What are you up to?"

"Talking to you."

"Ha."

"Writing an essay. What about you?"

"Talking to you."

What he always wanted to say—what he never said—was... *I love you.* Instead, he ummed and ahhed away the minutes, trying to collect the words together, so that in the end, all he ever got to say was...

"The money's about to run out, but I need to—"

And then it was back to his room, to beat himself up for never being able to find the words, and for being such a coward.

Josh lifted his head so he could see George's face. "Where have you gone?"

"Payphone in halls."

"Ah. Yes." Josh smiled at the memory of their mutual dumbness. It was a very expensive silence, and he still knew the number of that payphone off by heart. Until he moved into a shared house, Josh, too, relied on a payphone, and he would call at their agreed time, waiting with breath held for the line to ring out, sagging in disappointment at the repeating *beep-beep* of the engaged tone, but he would wait and try again, and keep trying until he got through. It seemed like only seconds would pass before his phone card was out of credit, and when he finally had a line installed in the house, the bills were astronomical. It didn't matter. He'd have given everything he possessed to hear George's voice. He almost had.

"He knew," Josh said. *"He always knew, and he kept it locked safely away, my secret that made a liar of him."*

"That's what people do when they love you."

Josh dwindled with the recollection for a few seconds before forcibly pushing it to the back of his mind. As always, the countless other thoughts and memories jostled to fill the space.

"You have bipolar disorder, Josh. It's a mood disorder, more commonly referred to as—"

"Manic depression," Josh snapped at the psychiatrist. *"I'm a graduate student of psychology. Don't talk to me as if I were an imbecile."*

Appalling behaviour, and he felt ashamed, although less so since he delivered his apology—several years too late, admittedly—only for it to be met with, *"Sorry. What was your name again?"*

George nudged Josh with his cheek, and he attempted a smile. George kissed him on the forehead. "Don't think about it."

Josh nodded to confirm he was trying to let it go. "Did you miss being near the coast?" he asked by way of distracting himself.

"When?"

"In Colorado."

"Not really. We had mountains and forests and springs. You kinda don't need the coast when you got all that."

"Kinda?" Josh teased.

George cleared his throat. He'd taken a lot of flak on the ranch for his English accent, though it was all done in fun.

"You Brits crack me up." Ray chortled.

"Why?"

"How'd ya say steerp?"

"Stirrup," George repeated innocently.

Ray burst into fits of laughter. "Awesome. OK, try another one…"

George soon learned to modify his pronunciation, not that it saved him much on the tormenting front, and it was far easier to pick up the lingo than to lose it again, so he'd received more of the same when he finally came home.

"Do I still talk like that?" he asked.

Josh shook his head. "Not anymore."

"You sound disappointed."

"I am a bit." Josh gave George a mischievous grin. "I kinda liked your cowboy thang."

"Uh-huh?"

"But rugged farmer works, too." Josh slid his hand inside George's T-shirt.

George sighed in exasperation and distracted himself by reading the satnav.

"How long left?" Josh asked.

"Ten minutes."

"Wow. That's quick."

"Are you surprised?"

They both looked at who was driving. The men in the front were too engrossed in their own conversation to notice they were the focus of their passengers' attention.

"No." Josh laughed. It had been a very speedy and uneventful trip so far, and he glanced behind him to check on Blue, who had been fast asleep the entire time.

George followed Josh's lead, chuckling at the sight of the big German shepherd dog curled up so tightly he looked half his size. "He's gonna be charging around like a crazy thing when we get there."

"He'll be fine once he's had a run on the beach."

"D'you think so?"

"I hope so." Josh lightly traced a fingertip up and down the taut skin of George's belly, trying to focus on the physical sensation and suppress his nervousness, wondering what it would be like, and also how many other wedding-night virgins had thought what he was thinking now. How many had shared his predicament?

"Have you ever...you know?" Eleanor asked.

"Erm...have I ever what?"

"Done it."

"Oh!" That 'it'. Josh blushed and stared hard at his English homework. "Why?"

Eleanor shrugged. "Just curious. No-one waits till they get married these days, do they? But I'm going to. Are you?"

"I suppose."

And he had, though not by reason of virtue. He wasn't saving himself for The One, nor had he denied his need because Man decreed it to be God's will. He simply did not 'need'. Desire was as vast and unknown to him as the ocean now coming into view, and he'd never so much as dipped a tentative toe. For on those two occasions when he'd felt a yearning that he didn't really comprehend, he had been far, far inland. Now they were arriving at the coast, together.

"You OK?"

"Hmm?" Josh looked around and realised they had stopped.

George laughed at him and opened the door. "Are you ready?"

Josh smiled and nodded. "Yes. I think I am."

To Have

MAKE LOVE TO me."

George looked down into Josh's eyes, studying the intent, the earnestness, the sacrifice. He shook his head. "No."

"I want you to."

"You don't."

"George, please—"

"No!" He moved away and sat on the end of the bed, staring out through the open balcony doors to the relative darkness of the bay beyond.

"This is our wedding night."

"Yes, Joshua, that's exactly my point. It's *our* wedding night."

Josh rolled across the bed and tried to put his arm around George, who didn't move away but tensed in resistance. "What's wrong?" Josh asked.

"You," George said curtly. "You are wrong. You say you want me to make love to you, when what you mean is you're prepared to *let* me make love to you because you think it's what I want. And it's not." He closed his eyes, his breathing momentarily paused by the realisation of what he'd said. "I don't mean that. What I mean is—"

"You were the one who said it! You said you wanted to make love to me *your way.*"

"And it was true, at the time. But not anymore."

"Please?" Josh implored, trying again to pull him close, but George shrugged him off.

"No," he repeated. He stood up. "I'm going for a walk." He left the room.

For a moment, Blue watched the door but must have realised George wasn't coming back for him. He lay down, with his nose on his front paws, and breathed out as if sighing.

Josh sat cross-legged, with his elbows on his knees and his chin on his hands, thinking. This wasn't the best start to their honeymoon—their first argument since they got together. And over what? He thought it was what George wanted. *The ultimate gift.* Now, he didn't know what to do. Should he go after him? Or wait until he calmed down and came back?

"You know, Blue, life's too short."

The dog turned a radar ear in his direction.

Josh bounced off the bed. "Come on."

Blue dutifully followed him out of the room, down and down the many steps onto the beach. It was as dark as it was going to be, a deep, purple twilight, nevertheless too dark for Josh to ascertain the direction George had taken.

"Which way?" he asked Blue, who immediately headed left. Josh followed a little more slowly, as the sand was soft and difficult to walk through, but soon he made out the dark figure sitting on a rock, a moody silhouette gazing out to sea. He walked over and slid across to sit next to him.

"Hey, you," he said.

"Hey," George replied, continuing to stare into the distance.

"Can we talk about this, please?"

"Yeah, I think we probably need to."

"Do you want to go first?"

"Not really."

"Fine. Then I will." Josh shivered. "That wind's cold." He snuggled closer.

George put an arm around his shoulders. "Better?"

"Lots." Josh examined George's profile. "We agreed to compromise, didn't we?"

"Isn't that what we've been doing?"

"I suppose. But it seems to me you're the one doing all the compromising."

"That's not true," George argued. "Being close doesn't require sex. I didn't understand that when I said I wanted to make love to you. I love what we have, and I love what we do."

"But it's not what you need, and—"

"I'm fine with it," George interrupted.

"Well, I'm not, and I always hear you out. Now it's my turn. So please, will you just listen to me?"

George sighed. "OK."

"See, I can't win. I offer to give you this, and you dismiss it because it's not what I want, and you're right. It isn't what *I* want, but it is what I want to give you. Then, when I do want it for real, you dismiss it as a symptom."

"Isn't that what it is?"

"If it were an itchy rash on my back, would you ignore my request that you scratch it for me?"

"It's hardly the same."

"Why isn't it? You want me to tell everyone the truth about my mental health, for what reason? Because it's nothing to be ashamed of? To reduce the risk that I might hurt myself?"

"For both of those reasons. And because it's part of who you are."

"Right. It's part of me, so it's part of us. And we have to accept that."

"I already did."

"No, you haven't accepted it. Not really," Josh countered. "You've taken on the responsibility of keeping me grounded or scraping me off the floor as need be, and yes—at some point, I am going to tell people, because you shouldn't have to do it on your own. I hadn't realised how hard it was for you, until…"

Josh was unsure how best to describe the horrendous weekend they had endured a few months earlier. They had both been ill, and George had tried to talk to him about it many times since, desperate to get a contingency plan in place, in the event that it happened again.

"When you built the snowman, you mean?" George asked.

Josh closed his eyes, attempting to block the memory. He felt ashamed and guilty for having forced Blue to go walking through the snow, and for being unable to care properly for George, when George always looked after him. It wasn't a compromise; it was plain unfair, and somehow, he had to make George see it from his perspective. He tried again.

"I need to get it back under control. Maybe I was in remission until last year, I don't know. Maybe we wouldn't even have ended up together at all if I'd still been on lockdown. We're here now, and I wouldn't change that for anything, but something has to give. It's not right that you're constantly worrying about me being ill whenever you're not there or when you're ill yourself."

George turned and met Josh's gaze as best he could in the dwindling light. "You don't have to tell people if you don't want to, like you don't have to let me make love to you."

His intention had been reassurance, but the outcome was quite the opposite. In fact, that was all it took to tip Josh over the edge. He shot to his feet, no longer able to hold back his anger and frustration.

"I've had enough of tiptoeing around this," he snapped.

"Fine," George snapped back. "Let's get it out in the open, shall we?"

Josh folded his arms and turned away, watching the last of the sunset dying into the sea.

George shook his head in furious disbelief. "This has nothing to do with telling everyone. This is about me saying no. After everything we went through last year, you still think if we don't consummate this relationship, someday I'll get tired of being rejected and leave. That's what this is about, isn't it? Like when you saw me talking to that guy in the pub and got yourself in such a state you threw up. It's just bloody stupid."

"Is it any more stupid than you getting jealous when I flirt with other people without realising it?"

"I get jealous because you never flirt with me, not because I think you're going to leave me! Your question in your vows—why did I choose you? Because you are everything I need. I don't need anything or anyone else. I married you. I love *you*."

"But it's not enough."

George's temper was threatening to take him over. He wanted to yell. He wanted to cry. He wanted to throw himself on the sand and beat his fists. He didn't. He held his breath, pushed the scream silently into it, let the wind take it from him. He studied the heavens, watching the stars begin to appear as he spoke.

"When we were at Dan and Adele's engagement party and I said I wanted to make love to you, what did you say?"

"I don't know."

"Yes, you do! You said that's what we'd been doing, and you were right. Whether we're playing video games or giving each other a massage or just kissing, that's *our* way of making love, and it doesn't need sex to make it complete. You don't even want it unless you're manic, and the rest of the time it's an act. And that's OK. I love you, and it makes me feel special, that you'll do that for me. I appreciate what a massive compromise it is, and I will not take advantage of you when you're ill or because you think you have to do this for us to be normal or to stop me from leaving. I'm not going anywhere."

Josh took a moment to breathe before he spoke, to make sure he was in control. He turned back to George and quietly corrected, "Hypomanic. Not manic. There's a difference. I know what I'm doing."

"But it's still part of your illness."

"No. It's part of *me!*"

George tried to swallow the tears, but he couldn't and covered his face with his hands. They'd come this far, they had to see it through, sort it out once and for all, but he didn't know if he had it in him, not after what happened the last time.

Josh could see and feel his pain, and he softened. He stepped closer and gently took George's hands. "Stand up."

George sniffed and shook his head.

"Come on, get up. Walk with me. We won't shout as much if we're walking."

George allowed himself to be pulled to his feet, and they set off, drifting slowly down towards the wash, still holding hands, talking about things that couldn't hurt them: the sudden and extraordinary brightness of the stars in the milky-blue sky; the peacefulness of the distant turn of the ocean and the ebb of traffic; the warmth of the sun that still lingered in the sand as it pushed up between their toes. It was a means of preparing to reconvene their discussion on more reasonable terms. Blue plodded along beside them, occasionally racing off after a gull engaged in a spot of late-night fishing or stopping to inspect a piece of seaweed.

The trouble was they were both so frightened of this thing, they only dealt with it when they had to and spent most of their time skirting around it in a superficial way, discussing diagnostic criteria, the pros and cons of treatments, the stigma of wearing the label. They talked about it as if it were a despised distant relative who took it upon themselves to visit occasionally, an uninvited and unwelcome intrusion. At such times, they would crank up the hospitality, as it were, tolerate behaviour from each other they might challenge in the normal course of events, and postpone dealing with any disagreements until the visitation was over. Now, they had to meet it head-on instead of turning the other way.

"Tell me how it feels," George said, after many minutes passed of walking in silence. "The hypomania. What's it like?"

Josh considered the question. He could give the answer he ought—claim that it was awful to feel out of control, lament the dreadfulness of insomniac nights and trying to keep track of a hundred thoughts at once—or he could answer truthfully. No lies. No secrets. That was the deal. He turned his head and watched George looking down at the impression of their footprints in the sand. He was waiting and listening. *Best give him something worth listening to; the truth it is.*

"Most of the time, it's incredible," he said. "When I was studying, it was like I could see the beginnings and ends of theories, how they connected, where they intersected, a massive web of ideas I could almost touch, become trapped and tangled within and never want to escape. Even now, it makes me feel like a genius, invincible, no-one else can possibly know as much as I know because they don't understand or see the world the way I see it.

"And it's bright and sharp. Everything looks so clear, so focused. The vividness of colours, smells—everything— is impossible to describe. It is the ultimate high, beyond euphoria. I can't explain because there are no words for it. It's Christmas morning, acing your exams, riding a roller coaster, falling in love—every good thing you've ever experienced all in one hit. The insomnia, as you call it, isn't insomnia when I feel like this. I don't need sleep, and I don't want it, because it would be such a waste when I could be doing so much else.

"But then there's the cleaning and house clearance. That's not so great. Everything looks and feels dirty and wrong. I have to fix it or replace it or get rid of it, and I have to do it right away. I've destroyed so many things that I wanted to keep when there was no-one around to question if it was really what I wanted to do.

"I dug a massive hole in the garden one time." Josh shook his head in embarrassment at the recollection. "I'd decided I was going to have a pond, maybe get some carp like Dan. I must've called him a dozen times in the space of an evening. Afterwards, I couldn't face filling it in again, so I left it like that for almost two years, pretending it wasn't there, until some old guy came round, looking for odd jobs. Anyway, if I get that far, which thankfully isn't very often, then that's the point at which I usually realise what's going on, so I know I'm crashing soon.

"As for the hypersexuality...I guess, for me, it's more like the average person's sex drive. I know lots of people end up doing really stupid, dangerous things—having affairs, sleeping around, doing stuff they wouldn't normally do. I've never felt like doing any of that. And it's strange thinking about it when I'm at baseline, because I can't believe how intense the feeling is. I want you so much that I have to clamp my teeth together to stop myself from saying what I'm thinking. It's dirty, in a pornographic way. God, it's embarrassing to remember afterwards. And I just want to touch you all the time, for you to touch me, for you to..." Josh stopped talking and felt himself blush. It was now too dark to see each other properly, not that it mattered. He didn't need to see to know George was smiling.

"I'm kind of glad you've never come out and said it. I'd probably laugh."

"Yes, you would. But the thing is, what I was trying to tell you before, and what I keep trying to tell you when it happens, is that I might not know why I'm doing it, but I do know what I'm doing, and it doesn't make what I want or need any less valid."

"And do you want me to take notice of everything you say you want or need when you're having an episode? Like when you plead to be left alone, or tell me you want medicating, or demand to go to the hospital?"

"I understand what you're saying, but—"

"Do you? You want me to make judgements on your behalf, and I will always do that to keep you safe, but the rest of it? You can't pick and choose. Either I'm going to do as you ask or ignore it. Which will it be?"

George stopped walking. Josh didn't.

"It's not that easy, is it?" George called after him. "Keep the hypomania and throw away the depression. That's what you really want."

Josh turned back. "Wouldn't you?"

"I can't answer that," George said, exasperated, desperate for this to end. They could go around and around forever more and never reach an understanding. The hypomania was addictive, Josh had admitted that, but whichever state he was in made little difference. For George, it was exhausting. He stepped off again, and they continued to walk side by side.

"You know I love you, yes?"

"Meaning?"

"Meaning that it's bloody hard work sometimes. It might be the ultimate high for you. It's not for me. It's damage limitation, but I love you and it's part of you, and I'm not asking you to change or get treatment or anything like that. Maybe you *were* in remission all those years. Or maybe you just got really good at hiding it. Whatever, I would rather have you the way you are now than go back to how it was."

"I'm glad about that," Josh said. "And thank you."

"For what?"

"I know it would be easier for you if I was on mood stabilisers."

"Oh, yeah. Obviously, I married a crazy genius for him to turn into a zombie."

"I'm not saying I'm going to."

"Corny as this might sound, I respect your right to choose."

"Right to choose?" Josh laughed sardonically.

"What I mean is, who's to say it's wrong to have the mega-highs you do? No-one should be allowed to take that away from you, even if it does mean I've got to stick to you like glue till you come out the other side." George stopped walking again and turned Josh to face him. "Please don't go on mood stabilisers. Not unless you really, truly want to."

Josh shook his head. "I won't. I don't need them—most of the time. I'm lucky. I can still function, and I can moderate my mood if I try hard enough. In fact, when I was on lockdown, it was totally under my control, until The Dream."

"Well, I think we might've figured out what that was about, huh?"

"Really?" Josh asked coyly. "What's that then?"

George laughed and kissed him lightly on the lips but then became serious and kissed him again, harder this time, yet with innocent intent. He pulled him close. "I made you a promise."

"You made me lots of promises today," Josh teased.

"You know what I'm talking about. But I accept what you're saying. I think I understand a little better now. And I'm sorry."

They were level with the hotel and started to walk up the beach towards it.

"I'm sorry too," Josh said, putting his arm around George's back. "I'm going to talk to Sean when we get back. Try to establish equilibrium."

"If it's what you want."

"It's what *we* need."

George shrugged. It wasn't his call.

"So," Josh hedged, "does that mean at some point we get to do it your way?"

George let out an exaggerated sigh. "Ask me the next time you're hypomanic."

To Hold

DAYLIGHT BEGAN GENTLY flowing in a little before four-thirty, and by five, the deep-pink glow of dawn eased its way across the sky, stretching into the ocean, chasing away the inkiness of night until it disappeared into the horizon.

A little after six, George found Josh sitting on the wooden deck of the balcony, cross-legged and bare-footed, arms loosely circling his knees, his hair lifting in the already warm morning breeze, his cheeks lit peachy-pink by the shimmering, distant reflection of the newborn sun. George crouched beside him and kissed him on the head.

"Good morning," he said, and almost lost his balance. Josh grabbed his arm to steady him.

"Good morning," he replied quietly.

George sat by his side and looked out, dazzled by the brilliant-orange light dancing across the surface ripples of deepest blue. "Wow. It's beautiful."

"It is, too," Josh agreed.

George turned and gazed at him, overpowered by the sudden and repeated realisation of their togetherness. "So are you."

Josh smiled but didn't say anything.

"How long have you been awake?" George asked.

"Not long. I wanted to listen to the waves. High tide was a couple of hours ago. And it was so loud, but such an incredible sound. I think I could live somewhere like this."

George turned his attention back to the ocean. "I think you might be right."

"Couldn't you?"

"Um, well..." He frowned. "If it was something you wanted to do, then I guess I'd get used to it. It's a bit quiet, although I liked that on the ranch. I don't know. I suppose, if you really—"

Josh leaned across and kissed him. "Shush." His whisper merged with that of the receding tide. He took hold of George's hands and shifted position so he was within George's arms. "Are we OK?"

"Yeah. We're OK."

"That's OK, then," Josh said and they both giggled. "What do you want to do today?"

"Eat breakfast."

"And then?"

"Dunno. I'll tell you after breakfast. I wonder if they have strawberries. I want strawberries. And melon. And pineapple. Do you think they'll—"

"I don't know," Josh interrupted. "You could've just said you wanted fruit."

"But I don't want any old fruit, I want—"

"Strawberries."

"Yeah." George became quiet, enjoying the moment, sitting with Josh—his *husband*—on a balcony, overwhelmed by the view, both near and far.

"I'm going for a shower," Josh said and moved to get up. George pulled his arms tighter around him. "Or I can stay here." He settled back against George's chest and sighed, although he could no longer stare out to sea; Blue had come to join them and was sitting directly in front, staring out to sea himself. Josh couldn't reach to stroke him, so he rubbed him with his toes instead. The dog flopped onto his side and rested his head on Josh's knee.

"I went to see a fortune teller when I was at uni," George said, apropos to nothing, it seemed.

"Why?"

"Emotional blackmail. There was a girl on our course—one of only two girls, actually—and she wanted to go and see this guy. Can't remember his name now, but it was a fairly ordinary name, not like that loon Adele had us going to see."

"Gary the Russian, you mean?"

George chuckled. "Yeah, him. So, anyway, no-one else would go with her, so I agreed to."

"They must see you coming, those pretty girls," Josh teased.

"I didn't say she was pretty, and as I remember it, I wasn't the one who insisted going to see Gary the Russian would be *fun*."

"I meant Sophie," Josh clarified. "She's very beautiful."

"She is," George concurred with a smirk. The entire conversation was a wind-up. "Is that a tiny bit of jealousy, Joshua?"

"Ha!" Josh lightly elbowed him in the ribs. George mouthed an 'ow' and nipped his ear in retaliation. "So was she pretty?" Josh asked.

"I guess so, in her own way. She looked like Bertie, now I think on, though a bit taller and broader."

"Bertie. I wonder how she's doing. I liked her. She was... colourful."

George laughed, recalling the one and only time they'd met Andy's very short-term girlfriend with her pink and black hair and accidental strip routine. "Yep, colourful would be the word for it."

"What did he say, then, the fortune teller?"

"He said he could see marriage and children coming into my life, but later on, when I was older, probably before I was forty."

"Ooh, spooky." Josh affected a mock mysterious tone.

George tutted. "The thing is, when he said it, I almost laughed in his face. But look at us now, not that I'm suggesting his prediction had anything to do with supernatural ability. What I mean is, I always wanted this, and hoped for it, but I never, ever thought it would happen." That realisation hit

George again; he made a little squealing sound and squeezed Josh. "We're together!"

"Ouch!" Josh said, laughing. "Are you ever going to stop doing that?"

"I hope not." George grinned. He leaned forward and kissed his cheek. "I love you. Have I ever told you?"

"I think you might have mentioned it once or twice, yes."

"Good." George settled back against the wall and returned his gaze to the sea. "Are you going for your shower soon?"

"Breakfast," Josh said knowingly. "Always food, isn't it?"

"I'm starving."

"All right. I'll go and shower."

"Do you want me to come?"

"No. I think I'm going to be just fine today."

George released him, and he went inside.

To make sure, Josh grabbed everything he needed and showered with his eyes closed. It wasn't the easiest thing to do in a strange bathroom, but it worked, because he was finished in less than ten minutes and, with the temperature outside rapidly rising, opted to leave his hair to dry naturally.

By the time George was showered, Josh was dressed and ready, which, he assumed initially, was why George had stopped dead in his tracks when he emerged from the bathroom, still wet and with a towel draped around his waist.

"Yes, all right. You've made your point," Josh said, balling the other towel and chucking it at him. George still remained where he was, statuesque. "What's the matter?"

"Just admiring the view." He attempted a breezy tone, but the tension in his throat gave him away. Josh was dressed differently than usual, which George found attractive enough, but what he was wearing now…

"I throw on a pair of linen trousers and a loose shirt and it turns you on?"

"You have no idea, Joshua." George exhaled slowly and edged his way between Josh and the bed, knowing exactly what was going to happen. He closed his eyes and went with it.

"This is not good," he said, looking up from his new position: lying flat on his back with Josh sitting on top of him.

"I think it is." Josh dipped his head until their lips touched.

George reached up and brushed Josh's hair back so he could see his eyes. "I want breakfast," he pleaded.

Josh grinned wickedly and slowly slid sideways, allowing his trailing thigh to drag across George's lower body. As soon as he was free to move, George bolted up and sat on the edge of the bed.

"Man, that was close." He delayed for a minute or so before he got up and put on his clothes. Josh remained where he was, following George's every move with his eyes, which made George smile.

"I really don't have any idea," Josh said quietly, crossing his legs and pulling his feet up underneath him. George paused and watched him. Josh brushed his knees and kept his eyes lowered. "You're the only person who's ever found me physically attractive."

"I doubt that, somehow."

"It's true."

George sat on the bed and took Josh's hand. "Well, even if it is true, it doesn't mean you're not."

"It's OK," Josh assured him. "I make up for it with intelligence." He looked up and smiled, but it wasn't genuine. "I know people are attracted to you. I think they sometimes wonder why we're together."

"That's crazy."

"Is it? You're tall, rugged, tanned, fit. What am I? A short, scrawny, washed-out dweeb."

"Five nine is hardly short."

"But you didn't deny the rest of it."

"OK. We'll deal with the important one first. You're not a dweeb."

"I am. Always have been. When we were at high school—"

"You mean, when we were at the high school you started a year early because you're a genius? Is that the same as being a dweeb? Because if it is, then yes, you're right."

"But you were all so confident, while I was—socially inept."

"You were shy and picky about who you socialised with, that's all. As for being washed out—"

"I burn so bloody easily."

"That's what I was about to say," George continued. "I remember once, when we went on a bike ride, and before you say we used to do it all the time, this one was special. I was thirteen, so you must've only been twelve, and we stopped under the viaduct, to get out of the sun, because you were going to burn. You were lying on your back, with your knees up, on the concrete slope running down to the canal bank.

"And I remember sitting there, looking at you and thinking, 'I want to kiss you.' You were sucking a lollipop, swirling it around your mouth with your tongue, and you turned and asked me a question, and I didn't hear a word you said because the longer I watched you, the more I wanted to kiss you. I wanted it more than I'd ever wanted anything.

"That was the first time, and it happened so often after that. It felt like I spent my life daydreaming about kissing you. All the times I got told off in maths for not paying attention? That was your doing. And you never showed any interest in me—not like that, so we just went on being friends, and I kind of felt a bit of a fraud. I hoped maybe one day you'd look at me the same way, but it didn't happen.

"When I was a teenager, full of raging hormones and sexually and *physically* attracted to you, that was really tough to take. Now? I'm OK with it. I still want to kiss you. You still turn me on. Especially when you wear clothes I can see through." He grinned.

Josh looked mortified. "By which I mean I can see your outline, not the detail. And it's beautiful. Lots of men our age would love to have a body like yours. But they don't always look at you because you don't give off the vibe. You don't flaunt it."

"I don't know how."

"And that suits me just fine." George got up off the bed. "It's all the more for me. Although I think they might look at you today, because you're definitely giving off something." He pushed his feet into his shoes and walked over to the door. "Come on." He held out his hand.

Josh got up and took the offered hand. "So I'm not a dweeb?"

"You're not a dweeb." George kissed him. "A geek, maybe."

Josh pushed him away playfully; George laughed and pulled him close again.

"But the most gorgeous geek in the world," he said. He checked he had the keycard for their room. "Won't be long, Blue," he called back to the dog, who was looking very cool and relaxed, lying by the open balcony door, and hardly even turned to watch them leave.

They were staying in a newer building, aptly named the 'Ocean Wing' and attached to the main hotel, which was where the restaurant was located. It was now after eight o'clock, and breakfast was served from seven-thirty until ten, so they came across quite a few people, mostly dressed in shorts and vests or T-shirts, heading out early to get in a day's sightseeing and return in time to catch the next incoming tide. As they greeted each other and continued on their respective routes, Josh looked down at his and George's hands, still entwined and with not even the slightest attempt at resistance.

"I'm impressed," he said.

George shrugged. "I'm not ready to take on the world yet, but after what we've talked about, I think I can probably deal with a little Cornish cove." He lifted their hands and kissed the back of

Josh's. "Aside from which, we're newlyweds on our honeymoon. Aren't we supposed to do mushy stuff like holding hands?"

"Good morning." A woman in formal blacks and whites greeted them with a smile as they arrived at the restaurant. "Can I have your room number, please?"

Josh gave her the number. George was too busy eyeing up the breakfast choices on the long, buffet-style counters to listen to the same information now being imparted.

"I'm going to get some coffee," Josh said and broke away.

"OK," George replied. "I see fresh fruit." Off he went. Josh poured two cups of coffee and selected a bowl of muesli from the variety of cereals; he was seated and eating whilst George was still pondering his own choices. After several minutes more, George arrived at the table with a bowl filled with red and black berries.

"What's that?"

"Berry compote. That's a typical middle-class name for something—compote. What does it even mean? And before you tell me it's French for 'mixture', I know that, but why not just call it berry mixture? Anyway, I don't know if it's got strawberries in it. Looks more like raspberries and blueberries to me. Oh, well. I think I'm gonna have some fruit salad after this. That didn't have strawberries in it, either, but it's got grapes and pineapple. What's that?" He nodded at Josh's bowl.

"Muesli."

"Cool. Might have some of that too."

"And full English after that, no doubt."

"Depends on whether I'm still hungry. And how the eggs are cooked. Did you notice? I didn't think to look. I wonder if they're fried or poached? I'm definitely not in the mood for scrambled. I know they had hardboiled eggs. They were next to the fruit and yoghurt. That'd be all right, I suppose."

Josh rolled his eyes. "If you stopped talking and ate your berry *mixture*, you could go and find out!"

George grinned and did as he was told, although judging by his face, the berries were a little more sour than he'd been expecting.

"I never used to talk this much," he said, screwing up his nose. "That's really sharp," he explained, unnecessarily.

"Yes, you did. You've always talked a lot."

"I think it's since I came back from America. Why d'you think that is?"

"Assuming you're right, and you're not, maybe it's too much time on your own?"

"Maybe." George stopped to poke a seed out of his teeth with his tongue. "Although I was only on my own at night, really, up until Joe. You know what I think?" Josh gave him a questioning look. "I think it's nerves."

"Are you serious?"

"Totally."

"I make you nervous?"

"No." George scooped the remainder of the berries up with the spoon and crammed them into his mouth. "It's quite nice once you get used to the tartness." He inspected Josh's muesli. Josh moved his hand out of the way. George took a spoonful.

"So, what are you nervous about?"

"Dunno. I'm gonna go get some of that muesli."

Josh watched him wander off towards the cereal counter. Somehow, he doubted George's talkativeness was at all to do with nerves. If anything, he talked less when he was worried or anxious. More likely, he was trying to fit in as much as he could before the person he was talking to interrupted or stopped listening, although there was more to it than that, and Josh was beginning to see what it was. He experienced his 'a-ha' moment at the same time as George arrived back at the table with an enormous mountain of muesli spewing milk from its summit, like an anaemic, glutenous volcano.

"My, that's a lot of muesli," Josh said, finishing the last mouthful of his own, comparatively minuscule portion.

"I checked out the cooked breakfast, and it looks great and everything, but I'm in the mood for cereal this morning. Not sure why. Maybe it's the weather." George used the bowl of his spoon to flatten the heap of oats and dried fruit so that it was drenched in milk and lifted a massive spoonful to his mouth. He sank into his chair and sighed. "Mmmm."

Josh shook his head and laughed. "You're a very strange man."

George grinned and mumbled around his breakfast, "I'd have to be. I married you, didn't I?"

Josh stuck out his tongue at him. "You get on with demolishing your muesli mountain. I quite fancy some bacon and toast." He lifted his coffee cup, draining it in one go. "And more coffee."

By the time he returned, George had eaten his way through most of his muesli and eyed the bacon and toast covetously. Without a word, Josh pushed his plate across the table and went to get the same thing again. He had to queue for it the second time around.

The dining room was busy, and the diversity of the residents astounded him. There were parents of all ages with their children, including babes in arms; there were many older couples, lots of surfer types, of course, and two other couples also on their honeymoons, although in both of the other cases, they had apparently informed the hotel of the reason for their stay, as shortly after they sat down, they were each brought a Buck's Fizz.

"The whole set," Josh observed, watching the two women at the table opposite giggling as they sipped at their celebratory drinks, with more of the same from the man and woman behind George.

"I couldn't drink Champagne for breakfast," George said through a mouthful of bacon and toast. "Too fizzy."

"Not with orange juice, it isn't," Josh responded vaguely. He was still watching the two women, totally enthralled by the absolute symmetry of their movements. It appeared that one of them was left-handed, the other right-handed. They wore their hair in an identical style, were of the same build and had similar, strikingly attractive facial features with defined, high cheekbones and bright, almond-shaped eyes. At precisely the same moment, they both realised he was staring at them and slowly turned their heads and glared. He smiled apologetically.

"Congratulations," he said. He blushed and turned his attention back to his breakfast.

George tutted without looking up. The two women started talking in hushed tones, every so often glancing across at Josh, while his cheeks burned redder and redder.

"Can you hear what they're saying?" he whispered to George.

"Yep," George replied, stuffing his mouth with toast. It was clear that Josh's curiosity had been misinterpreted, but George didn't want to get involved.

"What do I do? Should I apologise?"

"You didn't do anything to apologise for, did you?"

"No, but I was staring, which is very rude. I bet they're sick of people staring at them." He leaned in closer and mouthed, *They look like sisters.*

George nearly choked on his toast and tried to rectify matters with a gulp of coffee, which he ended up snorting out of his nose. Josh put his head down, and his hair, soft and untamed from drying naturally, flopped right over his face.

"Yes, they do," George uttered finally. He was still giggling. Meanwhile, the husband in the other couple, who was sitting more or less back-to-back with him, swivelled in his seat.

"What's your problem, exactly?" He directed the question at Josh. "Because it is your problem, not theirs."

"No, I, erm..." Josh began. He coughed nervously. "You misunderstand."

"I don't think he does," the man's wife chipped in angrily.

Josh looked to George for help. He was listening and chewing slowly, studying the pattern on the wallpaper whilst trying to remain solemn and inconspicuous.

"I'm sorry if I offended you," Josh tried. The women across the way were watching on, matching smug expressions on their faces. "And you also," he said to them. They folded their arms, and each raised a solitary and opposite eyebrow. Josh shrugged. "I don't know what else to say."

"It's a bit late for apologies, don't you think?" the woman behind George snarled.

George glanced at Josh, spotting the warning signs—a flicker of generally well-contained anger. He didn't lose his temper often, but when he did, he really went for it, and he looked set to blow. George needed to intervene, and quickly. Without a word, he got up and walked over to the two women across the way.

"Hi." He smiled as he approached. "I'm George." He turned back and winked, a twinkle of mischief in those sparkling green eyes. "And this is my husband, Josh. We just got married too. Whereabouts are you from?"

Josh listened on as the two women explained in a weird, dyadic start-and-finish-half-a-sentence-each form of speech, interspersed with overly-enthusiastic responses from George.

"Sorry about that," the man at the next table said. His wife repeated the apology.

"No problem. My fault." Josh flashed them a quick smile and sipped at his coffee. He could see that they wanted to explain the reason for their misunderstanding, although he was still annoyed they'd made assumptions. He was also taken aback by them not realising he and George were together; that had to be a first.

At any other time, Josh would have encouraged them to share. This morning, however, he wanted to be with George, just the two of them and Blue, and all the while they were sitting in here, the outside temperature was rising. It was a glorious sunny day, but they would need to get going soon if they were going to walk to the town before it became too hot.

George had come to the end of his diplomatic intervention and gave each of his new acquaintances a hug before returning to his own table, where he sat down, slurped the last of his coffee, and gave Josh a wide, beaming grin.

"Pleased with yourself?" Josh asked.

"Yep," George replied, still grinning.

"Are you ready?"

George nodded and waited for Josh to get up, then followed, putting an arm around his shoulder.

"I think you've made your point," Josh muttered out of the side of his mouth.

"Who says I'm making a point?"

They returned to their room, stopping long enough to put on sunblock, even though George rarely burned and Josh's clothing covered all but his face and hands. He'd also invested in a leave-in hair conditioner with a high SPF. The last time he spent a prolonged period in the midsummer sun, his scalp was so red and sore he'd been unable to touch it, never mind brush his hair, for three weeks.

Once they'd packed a large bottle of water and Blue's bowl into a rucksack, they were all set and headed out for the hour's walk that would take them to the town, following the southwest coastal footpath, which ran along the cliff, sometimes terrifyingly near the edge, so they were looking down onto rocks and beaches many feet below. Blue wandered close, unperturbed, whilst George kept his eyes covered and told Josh to let him know just as soon as it was safe to look again.

Josh was trying not to look himself and wondered if George had forgotten he was scared of heights. In any event, Blue had the sense not to get too close, even if he did seem to be taking great delight in frightening the life out of them by repeatedly tiptoeing to the very edge and peering over, then lolloping away with his tongue hanging out of the side of his mouth.

They arrived in town and quickly found the local market, traversing the makeshift aisles between the stalls with relative ease. It was still early enough in the summer for there to be few tourists, and George's massive breakfast deterred him from his usual routine of stopping to look at everything edible. He did love food, but he'd eaten enough that morning to last the entire day. Even so, they stopped off at a fruit and veg stall, immediately spotting the punnets of strawberries—much redder and more random in shape and size than the uniform, forced variety they were used to seeing in their local supermarket— and a multicoloured, multi-shaped array of melons as well as whole pineapples.

"Do you still want to get some?" Josh asked.

"Yeah. We can eat them this evening, while we're sitting on the beach and I'm sketching you." George grinned hopefully.

Josh pretended he hadn't heard the last part. He pointed to the takeaway containers of melon, mango and pineapple, cut into one-inch cubes. "They might be better, given the general absence of kitchen utensils in hotel rooms."

George nodded in agreement, and they bought a couple of punnets of strawberries and two of the boxes of pre-cut fruit, from there backtracking to an ice cream stall they'd passed a few minutes previously and eating their ice creams as they wandered around the rest of the market.

Many of the stalls were aimed at tourists, most stocked with cheap flip-flops and surfing gear, place-name T-shirts and mini-surfboard keyrings, while others displayed souvenirs geared towards the 'artier' visitor. Josh and George stopped at a stall that sold friendship bracelets constructed from braided, organically dyed threads, and intrigued the proprietor with their search for nine that were identical. It proved impossible, so they opted instead for a mix of colours and bought enough for 'The Circle', plus Sean, Sophie and Krissi.

Purchases made, they found a shady spot behind the stalls so they could put bracelets on each other. Josh struggled to tie the strands around George's wrist. They were quite fiddly, but it didn't help that his hands were shaking. When he finally got the bracelet tied, George took a firm hold of Josh's hands to still them.

"You don't want to wear one, do you?" he asked.

"That wasn't what I was thinking about. I was wondering whether Vincent gave me the cufflinks because he knew, and if so, how did he know?"

"He probably picked up on how self-conscious you are about your arms and figured you needed something to make you feel better about them."

"You think he could see that?"

"Yeah, I do. That's why you connected with him, and why he and Mrs. Kinkade hit it off. You've all got that semi-telepathic thing going on."

"It's not telepathy, it's—"

"Psychology. I know. But it's like magic to us mere mortals."

"Meta-communication, it's called."

"Geek."

"You're quite competent in it yourself."

"I doubt that."

"You just did it."

"Your hands were shaking," George argued.

"And you correctly interpreted why."

"Because I know you."

Josh narrowed his eyes. "And how can you tell I'm flirting when I'm totally unaware of it?"

"You touch people on the arm and stuff."

"Kris touches people all the time."

"But that's Kris. It's normal for him."

"But not for me?"

George shrugged. "That's what I said. I know you."

"OK." Josh glanced around the market, looking for a subject. He settled on an older woman, pulling a trolley behind her. "Tell me about her." He nodded in the woman's direction.

"Nope."

"Do it!"

George huffed, but Josh wasn't giving up.

"All right, she's local. She does her shopping here all the time." He watched her approach a stall and engage with the owner. "She likes cheese. It might even be her favourite food." They both continued to watch as the woman made her purchases: a selection of cheeses.

"How do you know she shops here all the time?" Josh asked.

"She knew where she was going, plus the stall owner knows her."

"And, pray tell, Doctor Watson, how you deduced that she was a cheese fiend?"

"Because it's a cheese stall, and she bought lots of it. Isn't it obvious?"

"Maybe. Or she could be having a dinner party."

"I doubt it. Not in this weather. And anyway, she's working class. The working class don't have dinner parties. They have people round for tea."

"Is that right?" Josh asked, although his expression said, 'I told you so'.

George laughed and grabbed him by his shirt front. "Stop trying to pull me into your geeky world."

"I hate to tell you, *ma moitié*, but you're already part of it." Josh held out his arm. "Now tie me up."

George looped the friendship bracelet around Josh's wrist, secured it, and took his hand once more as they made their way out of the market, stopping at the pet stall to buy a chewy bone for Blue, then onwards, up to the coastal path for the walk back to the hotel. They had to take it a little more slowly because of the heat, and between the three of them, they'd drunk all of the water, including a bottle they'd bought in the market. As such, it was a relief to finally step inside the hotel, out of the burning sun and into the coolness of their wing, although now that the sun was up above them, the same could not be said for their room.

It was a little after one o'clock, and they were hot and sweaty from the walk. George went straight to the shower whilst Josh opened the doors onto the balcony, letting in the ocean breeze— not gentle as such, but welcome and refreshing, in spite of its warmth.

George finished, and they swapped places. Josh tried to shower without wetting his hair, which was virtually impossible with the showerhead so high up and his eyes closed. When he emerged into their much cooler room, George was sitting on the bed, still in his towel, leaning back against the pillows, and reading.

"That's my book," Josh said, rubbing his hair until it was standing on end.

"A bit of light holiday reading, huh?" George kept his thumb between the pages, turning the cover so he could read out the title. "*What Life Should Mean To You* by Alfred Adler?"

"A psychoanalyst. Came up with the inferiority complex."

"One of Freud's buddies?"

"Not exactly. They fell out."

"Right." George made a point of acting disinterested.

"It's actually not that heavy going, so I thought, seeing as I haven't read it in a while..." George rolled his eyes. "Look, we can't all be sexy, sporty types!"

"You really do need those new glasses," George joked. "I mean, what difference will they make? You've got the rest of the geek thing nailed."

"Dan and Andy were waiting outside, so I just picked up whatever was closest to hand."

"Psychology books? Who brings psychology books on their honeymoon?"

Josh went to snatch it from him, but George lifted it above his head, trying to keep his arms stretched at the same time as being tickled and failing miserably. Josh caught the book and put it to one side.

"I don't think you're a geek really," George said.

"I *do* think you're a sexy, sporty type," Josh said. "Especially on the football pitch." George turned pink. "So…" Josh leaned across and picked up the bag containing the fruit they had bought, tipping it onto the bed. George looked pained.

"I'm not sure I want any at the moment. I'm still stuffed with breakfast and ice cream."

Josh uncovered a punnet of strawberries and picked out the smallest one he could find. "Not even this teeny, tiny, little one?" He dangled it in front of George's face. George screwed up his nose. Josh climbed onto his knees and crawled up beside him, still holding the strawberry. George closed one eye.

"Not even that teeny, tiny, little one," he said, shoving Josh's arm away.

Josh shrugged and put the strawberry between his teeth, moving closer. "How about we share?" He pushed his open lips against George's and bit the fruit so that half of it tumbled into his mouth.

"See, now *that's* sexy," George said. He couldn't take his eyes off Josh, who selected another strawberry and held it with his lips.

As their mouths came together, the fruit passed from one to the other and back again before George bit into it. The released juice trickled down his chin. Josh caught the drip with the tip of his tongue and traced it back up to George's lips.

"Hell, that's sexy," he muttered, with difficulty, around the probing tongue. He closed his eyes and was both relieved and disappointed to feel Josh moving away. A second later, he was neither of those things and jumped at the sudden cold spot on his chest. He looked down.

"Oh God." Beyond that, he was lost for words.

Slowly, Josh ran the cube of watermelon across George's chest, stopping to circle first one nipple, then the other, and downwards, leaving a wet trail behind that he followed with his lips. Lubricated by its own juice, the watermelon continued to slide unaided. Josh chased it and caught it with his mouth. George remembered to breathe.

"Hmm, let's see if honeydew is as juicy," Josh murmured, lifting a cube of the pale, fleshy fruit out of the box and starting over. George inhaled sharply. "Cold, is it?"

"Nope. It's really, really hot. I think you should probably— oh, sweet…" George could go no further because, it turned out, honeydew was just as juicy, and this particular cube had made it as far as the towel around his waist—or where the towel had been a moment ago.

"Think I might try the pineapple next." Josh reached into the box and fished out a chunk, which he positioned on top of George's belly button. The motion of his rapid breathing sent it tumbling to the side. It almost reached his hip before Josh caught it with his mouth.

"Or maybe the mango?" Josh placed a cube on each of George's nipples. The fruit stayed exactly where it was, and Josh shook his head. "Too sticky." He removed one of the cubes with his lips.

George studied the ceiling and breathed out very, very slowly.

"I think you should have this piece." Josh retrieved the second cube in the same fashion and delivered it into George's mouth.

George tried to speak, but with the mango and Josh's lips in the way, all he could manage was a muffled groan.

"What was that you said?" Josh kissed a trail back to George's nipples. "Just going to clean up this sweet, sticky mess." He sucked each one in turn.

George hurriedly swallowed the mango. "What I was trying to say is whatever you do, don't...do that! Josh!" Josh's thigh brushed up between George's legs, and he pulled his knees up, shaking his head.

Josh moved away, although he was far from done. Taking several pieces of watermelon in his hand, he tightened his grip—"This definitely works best"—and watched in delight as a mini waterfall cascaded through his fingers and down George's belly. He placed a fresh piece in the river of juice, where it freely slid down. This time, Josh didn't intercept until it reached its destination.

"Joshua! What are you doing?" George gasped and moved to push Josh's head away but quickly realised he didn't want to. The wonderful hotness of his breath after the cold fruit rendered him incapable of resisting. If his rational thought processes had still been active, he might have thought about bringing a halt to what was happening, if only to try to understand, because this felt different to all the times before, the 'going through the motions'. Very different. The pressure was perfect, and if he just... Then Josh stopped.

George glanced down, swallowed hard and closed his eyes, riding out another visitation of the coldness courtesy of a cube of honeydew. He was way past fighting to stop something he wanted to happen and eagerly awaited the return of Josh's lips, tongue, teeth...caressing, teasing, gently biting, sucking... harder and faster.

It was all becoming too much, and soon, George was propelled beyond the point where he could contain it, rocketing skywards, unable to hold back. He shouted out and put his hand over his mouth to muffle his cry, biting on his fist. He felt as if he were floating a mile in the sky; it was utterly mind-blowing. This was ecstasy; he'd truly experienced nothing like it before.

And then he was coming down to land again, suddenly, inescapably aware that he was lying naked in a hotel room, covered in fruit juice and saliva, and with the balcony doors wide open. Thankfully, it was a private balcony, and they were a good few metres above sea level.

Josh lifted his face and smiled.

George beckoned with his finger. "Could you come here, please?"

Josh clumsily draped the towel over George's lower body and crawled up the bed, where he fell into the crook of George's arm.

"Why did you do that?"

"Because I wanted to."

George's chest was drying in the breeze, and it was sticky to the touch.

Josh licked the patch closest to him. It was deliciously sweet. "I didn't expect it to taste like that."

George lifted his head and looked at him.

"Although you eat way too much garlic." Josh licked his lips.

"Must we analyse it?" George deflected, blushing.

Josh laughed and reached behind him, using touch only to find the strawberries and selecting the largest in the box.

George watched him, frowning in confusion. "You should've stopped."

"No, I shouldn't." He brought the lush berry to his mouth and sucked it. "You see, now you're spent, you won't misunderstand what I'm about to say, or my intentions, because I assure you, they are far from altruistic." He continued to run his tongue suggestively around the tip of the strawberry as he spoke. "You know I said there'd only been a couple of times when I wanted to erm…?"

"Hmm?" George queried cautiously.

"I don't necessarily mean *that*, George. In fact, I don't mean that at all, so you can stop fretting."

"OK. So?"

"So, make that three times?" Josh cringed a little with the embarrassment of admitting it.

George tilted his head to look at him properly. "You're not—"

"Hypomanic?" Josh finished the question and shook his head. "Just horny."

George turned on his side. "You got a food fetish or something?" he asked, unable to keep the smile off his face. He ran his finger down the opening in the front of Josh's bathrobe, tugging against the loosely tied knot until his belt came undone.

"Maybe. You're welcome to test that theory further."

George paused and looked him in the eye. "Not everything is a clinical trial." Josh grinned at him, but George still wasn't sure. "Seriously, what do you want to do?"

"I'm open to suggestions," Josh said breezily.

George thought for a moment and shrugged. "OK." He reached across and took something from the box. Josh was about to experience a replication of his own methods.

"Fuck, that's cold," he gasped as a piece of pineapple came to rest in the middle of his chest.

"You want me to close the door?"

"Whatever." Josh shut his eyes and lay back.

George kept watching him and slowly pushed the pineapple until it came up against an erect nipple. Josh held his breath. George waited for him to exhale and then encircled both the cube of fruit and nipple with his mouth. No response to that, he looked up again to find Josh still had his eyes closed and was chewing on his bottom lip. "Are you OK?"

Josh opened his eyes and bent forward, pulling George close and kissing him, using the pressure of his lips and the force of the kiss to propel him back down onto the bed, sucking and biting at his lips until George, too, was panting for breath.

"Josh, I—"

"Shh. Stop worrying, I'm fine. The pineapple was cold and your lips are—hot." He kissed them again. "Really, really hot." He repeated George's words, his voice trembling with urgency.

"Oh, you like hot lips?" George pushed Josh onto his back again and ran his open mouth down, blowing hot breath over Josh's chin, chest and onwards.

Josh writhed against him, letting out a high-pitched squeal as something cold landed on his belly. He glanced down in time to see the bright-red watermelon disappear into George's mouth.

"How about some of that juicy honeydew?" George suggested. He put a cube of the fruit in his teeth and dragged it across Josh's abdomen, smiling around the fruit as goosebumps popped up all over Josh's body.

Josh shivered, mostly due to the melon's lubricating effect rather than its coldness. He reached down and put his hand on George's head, guiding, holding, controlling, and then pulling back.

"Do you want me to stop?" George asked but continued at a slower pace.

"No. Yes!" Josh took a breath. "Can we do this together? It might never happen again, and I'd like it to be good for both of us."

"This is good for me just as it is."

"Please? I feel really self-conscious."

"And now he sees!" George raised his eyes to the skies in praise.

Josh drew his legs up. "I always did. I just didn't understand it quite so—intimately." He took slow, deep breaths, trying to control the anxiety and desire that had him shivering so violently.

"All right," George conceded. "But it might take me a bit longer." He crawled back up the bed, kissing every inch of exposed flesh along the way. Josh still had his arms in his bathrobe, and George anticipated he'd want to keep them there, but as their faces drew level, he wriggled his shoulders and eased his arms out, wrapping them around George's back and pulling him down on top of him.

"Although…" George rolled onto his side, taking Josh with him so they were lying next to and facing each other. Josh ran his hand down to George's waist, bringing it to rest on his hip. George mirrored his position, sliding his leg up until it was resting between Josh's thighs.

"I don't know what to do," Josh confessed.

"Go with your instinct. I'll follow." George shuffled closer and kissed him.

Josh returned the kiss and kept it going, falling into it, drinking in the sweetness of George's breath, the softness of his lips, the increasing tempo of his breathing, synchronous with his own. He felt himself moving in closer still, sliding on top of George, still without breaking the kiss, and pushing against him, George pushing back, all without any conscious effort. The motion was spontaneous, the rhythm accelerating of its own accord, skin against skin, a gentle friction, growing in speed and intensity, the heat flooding through him, through them both.

As Josh felt the crescendo begin within himself, so, too, did he hear George's breath catch, their lips parting long enough for the silent screams of their passion to escape, whirling around and around, spotlighted by wisps of sunlight sneaking into the room before being whipped away on the ocean's breeze. Josh collapsed in George's arms, panting, exhausted, fulfilled.

They stayed where they were for a long time afterwards, whispering I-love-yous and delivering tender kisses to lips, noses and fingertips, until their damp, naked bodies relented to the breeze.

"I think I might need another shower," George said.

Josh slowly pulled away. "Hmm, me, too." He glanced down and grimaced. "My bathrobe's, erm…" He blushed, and George chuckled.

"We'll find a launderette later. Let's go shower."

***

As the afternoon cooled into evening, George took Blue for a quick run along the beach, returning to find Josh sitting out on the balcony with an open book in his hands.

"Whatcha reading?" he asked, leaning down to kiss Josh's head.

"Mills and Boon."

George chuckled. "Still Alfred what's-his-face then?"

"Adler. I delivered a lecture on him at the start of the counselling course."

"I'm sure you did. But some of us only remember useful things, like where we've put our sunglasses." George frowned and looked around him, puzzled. "I was just wearing them."

"Try the top of your head," Josh suggested.

George reached up and removed them with a grin. "It's all this fresh sea air, I swear." He went back inside the room and took the tiny kettle to the bathroom. "I take it you want a coffee?" he called back.

Josh was too busy kissing Blue on the nose to reply.

George emerged from the bathroom and plugged the kettle in. "Was that a yes?"

"Yes, please," Josh murmured around the dog's muzzle. Blue flopped onto his back to have his tummy tickled.

George brought the coffees out, and they sat together watching the tiny black specks of surfers bobbing along the white frill of the ocean at the far end of the bay. It was a beautiful evening, with the descending sun cast in rich, warm orange. From their location, a yacht appeared as a stark, black silhouette, merging seamlessly into its own elongated shadow that stretched towards the beach. Andy had been right: this place was perfect.

"What do you want to do this evening?" Josh asked, exchanging his book for his coffee.

"I don't mind," George replied dreamily. "I'd be more than happy to stay right here and watch the sunset."

"Aren't you hungry?"

"A little. Why? Are you?"

"Starving."

George turned and looked at him. "You'll be telling me you want to go eat some fancy pasta thing next."

"Actually, that sounds amazing. Seafood in garlic butter. And loads of pasta."

"You're kidding me!"

"I'm not," Josh said very seriously. "What was that stuff you made at Christmas? That was some sort of shellfish, wasn't it?"

"Moules marinière. You didn't like it."

"I didn't say that."

"No, but you had your 'I hate this' face on."

"My what?"

George wrinkled his nose and pulled his lips tight together. "No, no, it's really nice, George," he muttered through gritted teeth.

Josh laughed at the impersonation. "I do not look like that!"

"You do! When you're pretending you like something when in actual fact you hate it, that's what you look like."

"I dispute that. And anyway, I don't *hate* anything. Dislike intensely, maybe."

"OK. If you say so."

"I do. Although if I'm having garlic, then so are you."

"That's a bit presumptuous, isn't it?"

Josh grinned and leaned across the arms of the chairs with lips pursed. George pretended to back off.

"You still expect me to kiss you?" he joked even though Josh's lips were already on his. Josh poked with his tongue. George allowed him in, and they continued to kiss for half a minute or so before he pulled away for real.

The entire situation bothered him, but he didn't know how to say so without it leading to another difficult discussion. As much as he'd enjoyed their passionate afternoon, it had created uncertainty. When they'd first got together, it had taken a little work, but they'd eventually established a line, a distinction between intimate behaviour that was overtly sexual and that which was not.

Initially, George had felt as if Josh's lack of arousal were some kind of rebuttal, but with much reassurance, he had learned to overcome the sense of rejection that he had created in his own mind. If he wanted to pursue sexual gratification, he only had to ask, although most of the time he was happy to do things the way Josh wanted because, inevitably, George became so aroused there was only one possible outcome, and they were both fine with that.

Likewise, he now recognised the warning signs of when Josh's hypersexuality was about to kick in and was fairly resistant to Josh's efforts to push him into doing things that, much as he wanted to, took advantage of his temporary poor judgement. After talking it through last night, George thought he could even go along with what Josh was suggesting—accepting his needs were real rather than merely a symptom—although he wouldn't know for sure until they arrived at that situation again.

In the absence of all the other crazy behaviour, Josh's desire had thrown him into a state of confusion, and there were so many questions racing through his mind he was finding it virtually impossible to keep his thoughts concealed—that really took some effort in Josh's company. He'd always been able to read everyone except George, but once Josh let him in, he essentially had a direct line to George's psyche.

"Don't worry," Josh said, right on cue. "It'll pass and everything will go back to normal."

George narrowed his eyes. "I might as well've said everything I was thinking out loud."

"Yes, you might just as well." Josh smiled and took George's hand. "And on the matter of only remembering useful things, I asked if you wanted a lick."

"Huh?"

"My lollipop? When we were lying under the viaduct."

"Oh."

"You were watching me so intently it made me nervous, so I tried to crack a joke to cover up, and, strangely enough, you just said, 'Huh?'"

"You wanna ask me again?" George said, moving in for another kiss.

"Will you answer this time?"

"Try me."

"Do you want a lick of my lollipop?"

Josh gasped as George moved down from his lips to his neck. Alas, the moment was lost to a loud grumbling from Josh's stomach.

George laughed. "Shall we go and eat first?"

In Sickness...

Four a.m.

G EORGE LAY LISTENING in awe to the roar of the high tide as the brightness of the midsummer dawn slowly filled the room through the part-open balcony door. Blue got up, stretched, rested his nose on the edge of the bed for a moment, and took himself off to lie in the breeze. It felt cooler today, but it was still early.

Josh stirred and rolled over. "Are you all right?" he asked sleepily.

"I'm fine. Listening to the ocean."

Josh moved closer and put his head on George's chest.

When they next awoke, still in the same position, it was almost seven o'clock. Josh rubbed his eyes.

"How amazing is sleep?" he said, as if it were the first time he'd ever experienced it.

George smoothed Josh's hair back from his face and planted a kiss on his forehead. "You are completely nuts, sometimes. Do you know that?"

"Only sometimes?"

"You slept well?"

"Very. I'm not getting up yet, so you can have the shower first if you like."

George put his arms around him and squeezed. "I'm staying right here." His belly started rumbling. "For now. Definitely the sea air."

Josh's belly joined in. "You might have a point," he said, squirming to try to stop it.

They stayed where they were, listening to the much quieter and, by now, well-receding tide, and talking about anything and everything—the journey they had made to be in this moment, together, wrapped in each other's arms. They laughed about their closest friends, and how long they had patiently watched from the sidelines, waiting for them to find each other. They marvelled again at the undiscovered secret wedding celebrations and honeymoon. They cried a little, too, and shared their fears in order to pool their strength.

George was dressed by the time Josh stepped out of the bathroom feeling a little dazed. He'd found it quite a struggle, unused to the sensual awakening of his body, and had chanced to look upon himself. George took hold of his hands and led him to the centre of the room, where he helped Josh find clothes and buttoned his shirt for him, all the while staring into his eyes.

"Why are you dressing me?" Josh asked.

"I can't bear to see you hating yourself. You are beautiful." He lifted Josh's arms and kissed each wrist in turn. "In every way. To me, you are beautiful."

"Something weird is happening to us," Josh said, the spark of life gradually returning to his eyes. "You've turned all romantic, and I've…" He lowered his face, suddenly bashful.

"After breakfast, Joshua," George said, moving closer, his intent to leave the lightest peck on Josh's lips, but Josh returned the kiss, hard, passionate—hungry. George rubbed his empty belly. It was protesting again, and Blue needed to go out first.

"You go and get food," Josh suggested. "I'll sort the dog out. You've done it plenty already."

George accepted. "I'll get the coffee poured. See you in a little while."

Josh and Blue headed down the steps to the beach, where they bumped into the women whom Josh had upset the previous morning. Today, they were dressed in white vest tops and blue cropped pants. They also had a dog—a little, white, fluffy thing with a black snubby nose.

"Morning." Josh offered them a smile. Blue was most intrigued by their little dog.

"Good morning," the women responded in unison. Blue had rolled onto his back in submission, whilst the other dog sniffed at him. The women laughed; Josh joined in.

"The size he is too! Come on, Blue. Get up."

Blue dutifully obliged and went tearing around in circles, the little white dog standing completely still and watching him.

"By the way," Josh said to its owners, "I'm really very sorry about yesterday morning. It was so rude of me to stare, but I was quite taken with how happy and, erm, together you are."

"It's OK."

"OK."

Josh smiled swiftly and called Blue back to him. Sorry as he was, they still freaked him out, although, he reasoned, their 'togetherness' was no different from the tendency he and George had to do or say the same thing at the same time, and it finally dawned on him that it was the reason why, over the years, they'd been asked so many times if they were in a relationship. It also triggered a bit of catastrophic thinking on Josh's part, as regards yesterday's misunderstanding, leading him to question whether there was any truth to the theory that marriage pushed people apart.

Those thoughts carried him all the way up to their room and back down again. He was in quite a state by the time he arrived at the restaurant, where George was tucking into a plate loaded with eggs, bacon, sausages and toast. Josh flopped into the chair opposite and picked up his coffee. George swallowed his current mouthful of bacon.

"Everything all right?" he asked.

Josh nodded. "I met the sister wives on the beach. They've got a dog. It's a weird little…" He shrugged. He didn't know the difference between a pedigree and a mutt.

"Pomeranian," George finished. "Bossy bugger too. We saw them yesterday evening."

"Oh, right." Josh sipped his coffee.

"You gonna get some food?"

"In a minute." He put his cup down again. He was still feeling a bit strange and couldn't figure out why—lightheaded and fidgety.

"What's wrong?" George asked.

"I don't know. I'm just—I'm frightened. George?"

"You think you're hypo?"

"Am I?"

"Nope."

"Are you sure?"

"Yep."

"OK." Josh picked up his cup again. He was getting a headache. Lack of food, he rationalised. "I'm going to get some of that." He pointed at George's plate and stood up but came over so dizzy he had to sit down again.

"I'll get it. You stay there," George said. "You want the same as me?"

Josh nodded. He felt helpless and a bit pathetic. On the plus side, his heart had slowed down, and he wasn't feeling quite so frantic. As his breathing returned to normal, he realised he'd had a panic attack. George came back with his breakfast.

"Better?"

"I think so." He smiled weakly.

So there was the next step in his conquest: to get past pathologising every little variation in his behaviour; to stop overthinking. George didn't seem unduly concerned by the fact he was acting differently.

A short while later, the couple with the Pomeranian arrived— minus their dog—and nodded a unified greeting. George and

Josh nodded back. They were nearly done with their breakfast, thus mostly avoided communication with the two women, who continued to talk in the same split-sentence dialogue.

Back in their room, Blue was lying on the balcony and didn't even bother getting up to greet them. It was a lovely morning—nowhere near as hot as the previous day—and they decided to go down onto the beach for a walk. Josh was feeling less restless but still not quite his usual self, such as he had a state of usualness these days.

The tide was a long way out, so they wandered amongst the rock pools, stopping to examine the creatures trapped within, paddling in the shallows and jumping out at the last second as Blue came tearing up to them and leapt right in, a perpetual tiny heap of sand on top of his nose. George sat on a rock and watched Josh attempt to roll up the legs of his trousers once more.

"Next time the girls buy me pants for the beach, I'm going to suggest they get the ones with straps and buttons to hold up the bottoms," he said, fighting with the wet, sandy fabric.

"I don't suppose they thought you'd be doing much in the way of paddling, to be fair."

"Good point." He sat next to George and glanced down at the shallow water rippling around their feet. "I've never been anywhere like this."

"Me neither." George took Josh's hand in both of his and kissed it. "I was thinking before, when we were having breakfast." He turned a little so he could make eye contact. "If this does turn out to be more than a spot of honeymoon euphoria…"

"So you do think I'm hypo?"

"No." George sighed. "I don't know, truth be told, because if you were, you'd be struggling to sit still. You'd probably be off making sandcastles or some other mad thing."

"I'm never going to live down building that snowman, am I?"

"Well, it's not generally the kind of thing a man in his thirties does on his own," George pointed out, trying to keep a light-hearted inflection in his tone.

Josh squeezed his hand. "You know, this is good. Talking about it like this. Maybe we need to get away more often."

"Yeah," George agreed wistfully. "It's just so hard to find the words."

"I had an idea about that." Josh slid down off the rock and waded through the water, stopping a few feet away. He turned back. George was watching him with such intensity it suddenly made him feel naked.

"Are you undressing me?"

"Um, maybe." George grinned. "What's this idea?"

"Synthesis of emotion."

"Huh?"

"It's a left and right brain thing. Your problem with words."

"OK?"

"Language is mostly processed by one side of the brain, yes?"

"If you say so."

"I do. Whereas emotion is bilateral."

"Can we do this in non-geekese?"

"Your brain is in two halves, called hemispheres, and most right-handed people process language in their left hemisphere, but it might be that your right hemisphere is more strongly activated…" George's eyes glazed over. "To cut to the chase, you were kind of there when you suggested your talkativeness is related to nerves, but it works both ways. I think that specific emotional situations cause you to develop a stammer."

"Well, why didn't you just say that?"

"Because it's too complicated to explain." Josh paused and frowned. "Actually, that's sort of a lie, but I didn't want to upset you."

"You want to start over and do it truthfully?"

"Yes. Are you ready?"

"I think so."

"OK. All of what I said was accurate, incidentally, but not necessarily in your case. I think the seizures you had last year and the stammer are both caused by the same kind of psychological block. It stops you from expressing your emotions in verbal form."

"This is gonna get Freudian, isn't it?"

Josh laughed. "No."

"So we won't be discussing my mother?"

"I promise."

"OK. Tell me more."

"Well, that's all, really. It's just a theory."

"Test it," George said. Josh walked back towards him and took his hands. "Go on. I know you want to."

"All right. Try this: tell me how you feel about Sophie."

"OK. Well, she's...err, Soph's a...friend? Not a friend, or at least..." He studied the sky and tried to think. "What it is, I mean, what we are..." He sighed and shook his head. "I can't—"

"Stop," Josh commanded. George smiled wanly. "I'm guessing you guys have a birth plan drawn up and everything?"

"We did it months ago online."

"Did you?"

"Yep. When we booked in for the antenatal classes, they gave us loads of leaflets detailing all of the options for home births, hospital births and birth plans other people have drawn up. Soph says she just wants to keep it simple—she's not into all the New-Age stuff of having music playing and whatnot. I think that's why we hit it off, you know? We're quite a lot alike on things like that. None of that pretentious nonsense, especially—"

"And stop," Josh said. George let go of the rest of what he'd been about to say. "We'll come back to that in a minute. Why don't you want to live somewhere like this?"

"Because I think it's too quiet and, well, the thing is that it's OK—I say it's OK, but I, err...oh, sod it!"

"Can you imagine living somewhere like this?"

George considered the view and nodded. "At first, it seems perfect—getting up every day and watching the sunrise, listening to the sound of the waves. But we wouldn't, would we? We'd be too busy working, and we wouldn't ever stop to appreciate it."

"That's very true."

"It's like when you go on holiday, you have all this time to—ah!" George chuckled to himself as he realised what was happening.

"Do you see?" Josh asked.

"Why is that?"

"In non-geekese, I think it's something to do with processing emotions visually. Like when you used the painting analogy for your vows. If you can visualise it, then you can vocalise it."

"Try another one."

"All right. Let me think." Josh had something in mind, but he wasn't sure how George would react. "OK," he said, watching him closely in case it went horribly wrong. "Don't tell me if you don't want to, but if you had to paint a landscape to depict your dad, what would it be?"

George answered right away. "That massive garbage patch in the middle of the Pacific Ocean. It's mostly hidden, but it's still there, under the surface, destroying marine life. Albatross chicks die because they can't digest the plastic, and it goes right the way up the food chain, causing disruption to the endocrine system of some species, because the chemicals produced by the polymers are mistaken for hormones. Then there's the pollutant effect of degrading—"

"In conclusion, then," Josh said, cutting him off midway through what was becoming a rant, "it's just a case of re-wording the question."

"You are so geeky," George said, encircling Josh's waist entirely with his arms and smiling up at him.

"Who was it who just detailed the effects of pollution on the endocrine system?"

"You're still geeky."

"And still you love me." Josh kissed the top of George's head.

"Yeah, I do."

"What colours would you use to express how you feel when I'm sick?"

"That brownish-grey you get when you rinse your paintbrushes."

"Nice!"

"It's all mixed up, is what I mean."

"Yes, I gathered as much. What about if Jake knew about it?"

"What's Jake got to do with anything?"

"He's your boss, and if you ever need to take time off work to look after me…"

"It's fine. I'll tell him I'm sick."

"We can discuss that. For now, just humour me?"

"All right. It's more kind of greenish? See, I know he'd be OK about switching my shifts around if I told him in advance, because I can tell, you know, when you're about to, um…so yeah. It would give us more freedom, I think."

"OK. You have my permission to tell him."

"Maybe we should talk about it some more when we get home."

"Will it make it easier for you if he knows?"

"Well, yes, but—"

"Then I'll tell the university and you tell Jake. It'll be one less thing for you to worry about."

***

They spent the rest of the day wandering between the hotel and the beach. For a while, they sat on the deck outside the bar and drank beer but went inside for the hottest part of the afternoon before strolling back along the beach to watch the kite surfers at the next high tide. George had brought his sketchpad, Josh, a paperback.

"What're you reading now?" George asked after half an hour of sitting in silence, both completely absorbed in what they were doing.

"Mills and Boon," Josh said, turning the page. George raised an eyebrow and carried on watching him. Josh glanced up. "You'd best not be drawing me."

"I'm not at the moment."

Josh frowned and continued to read. George lay down and shuffled over so his face was underneath the open book. He read the cover upside down.

"*How to Read Human Nature: its Inner States and Outer Forms*, by William Walker Atkinson."

"It's one of his earlier works, before he went religious."

"Sounds riveting." George pretended to fall asleep. Josh uncrossed his legs so that George's head fell between them. "If we were in our room, I'd be in a very useful place to do something about this."

"If we were in our room, I'd let you."

"You don't mean that, do you?"

"I do a little bit." Josh lightly squeezed George's shoulders with his knees.

George sat up again, side on. "Let's not look ahead. We can take it as it comes."

"It feels weird."

"Yeah, it would to you. Mr. Got-To-Have-A-Schedule-For-Everything."

"I am not like that!"

"You are."

Josh opened his mouth, about to protest, but nodded instead. "Yes. I am," he agreed. "And I'm also starting to burn."

George got up and pulled him to his feet. "Come on."

"What are we doing now?"

"Going back to our room, and then—let's go with the flow."

"We could go to the bar."

"We could."

"Or there's the place across the road. They have live music. We could go there."

"Yep. We could do that."

"Or maybe stay in and…"

George stopped walking and spun Josh around so he could kiss him. It wasn't just a light peck, either. He took his time, exploring Josh's mouth with his tongue, holding him close.

Josh pulled away and blinked in amazement. "There are people here who can see you," he pointed out breathlessly.

"Yep." George continued to smile at him.

"I guess we don't need to stay in, then."

"Like I said, let's just take it as it comes. But I think it's time we both came out for real, don't you?"

"I don't know if I'm ready."

"Which is why I want you to be sure before I tell Jake."

"I'm fine about that. Really, I am, but having a routine helps me keep it together."

"And stops you from being yourself."

Josh tried to turn away, but George wouldn't release him.

"I'm not saying you should completely get rid of it. You need it. I totally get that, but it doesn't mean we can't sometimes do things on the spur of the moment. What are you scared of?"

"That I'll embarrass myself, and you."

"How?"

"Like when I cried in front of everyone on my birthday. If I can't mentally prepare, how am I supposed to stay in control?"

"It's OK to have emotions."

"Normal ones, yes."

"Crying because you're happy is normal."

Josh examined him suspiciously. "I know where this is going."

"It's like when Data finds Spot—"

"I knew it! Bloody Star Trek again!"

George grinned at him. "OK. Start with this: I'm going to try to be more 'out' for you, and you're going to try and be a little more spontaneous for me. What d'you think?"

"Sounds like a reasonable compromise."

"Do I get to paint you yet?"

"No."

For Better, For Worse

THE NEXT MORNING, having been kept awake for much of the night by a particularly high tide battering the rocks below the hotel, they both slept in and had to go to breakfast before they showered or else they would have missed it, which had Josh stressing over the state of his hair.

George sat across the table, watching him try to spread marmalade on toast, pausing every few seconds to blow his fringe out of the way and becoming increasingly exasperated. It made George smile.

Josh glanced his way and briefly reciprocated. "Is it badly sticking up?"

"Nope." George's eyes strayed upwards as he answered.

"It is, isn't it? Oh, God. I'm going to eat this and go and sort it out."

George shook his head and continued to watch Josh.

"If it's not sticking up, why do you keep staring?"

"Because it's sexy. Bedhead. Unusually untame. I like it."

Josh huffed and blew at his fringe again. "I need to eat faster."

When they returned to their room, George took Blue down to the beach, leaving Josh to shower in peace, even though he was a little worried about doing so. Indeed, his concern preoccupied him to the extent that he was almost back at the hotel before he became aware he was being followed, sort of. He turned and looked behind him.

"Hi," he acknowledged the man who had been walking parallel to him but slowly moving closer the further along the beach they came. He was wearing knee-length khaki shorts and a pale-green vest top, his tanned, muscular physique on full display.

"Hi," the man replied with a smile. He nodded at Blue. "He's a beautiful dog."

"Thanks."

"How old is he?"

"About ten months."

"From a breeder?"

"No. Rescued."

"That's awesome. I bet he gets hot with all that black fur. How's he coping with the heat?"

"Not bad, so long as he's not out in it for too long."

"You staying in the hotel?"

"Yeah. You?"

"Up at the campsite." He nodded into the distance, beyond the bay.

George shielded his eyes against the sun, spotting the tents and caravans nestled amongst the hills. It had been a while—eighteen years, to be exact, ignoring Joe—but he had more than an inkling he was being chatted up.

"Are you here long?" the man asked. "Sorry, I'm Will." He held out his hand.

"George," he said and shook the offered hand. He didn't quite know what to do when his judgement might be way off, although he was pretty sure it wasn't.

Will fell in step with him as they continued to walk towards the hotel. "You into surfing, George?"

"No, although I've never tried. You?"

"Yeah. I come here for the surf every summer. I love it."

George nodded. He was close enough to veer off and did so, hoping Will would take the hint, but he didn't. Still, the conversation was innocent enough. The truth was if George had been single, or rather, in another dimension where he hadn't been in love with Josh for all of his adult life, he'd have quite happily gone wherever this subtle flirtation took him. Will was good company and seemed impressed that Blue was a rescue dog; from how he was talking and acting, he evidently liked dogs a lot. He was funny too, and despite his resistance, George found himself laughing at Will's jokes.

As they came up on the Ocean Wing, George noticed Josh standing on their balcony, leaning on the rail. Watching. The guilt devastated him.

"Well, it's been nice talking to you," George said, stepping as far away from Will as he could.

"And you," Will replied with a frown— understandably, as George must have seemed quite receptive. Will followed the direction of George's gaze, to the balcony.

"Oh. I'm sorry," he said, though he lingered in appreciation— again, understandable. What Will saw was precisely what George saw: a slim, good-looking guy, pale-blonde hair falling gently over his face, loose-fitting shirt billowing in the breeze, the sun lighting his profile from behind.

"Hey, it's OK," George said. "I'm flattered, but…" He held up his hand so Will could see his ring, which was perhaps more to do with laying claim to Josh; he'd noticed that look in Will's eye. So he found Josh more attractive? Either way, it was a compliment.

"Why didn't you say something?" Will asked.

"Because I didn't want to…um…" George shrugged.

"I understand," Will said. "I live in a little village in Sussex. I know what it's like."

"Yeah, well, no harm done." George glanced up at Josh again, whose thunderous glare made a liar of him.

"Tell your husband I'm really sorry," Will said. "Good to meet you."

With that, he waved and jogged away, past the hotel and up a path cut into the cliff.

George looked once more towards their balcony; Josh had gone inside. He called Blue and headed back to their room, with a good idea of what he'd find when he got there.

***

"Hey," George called lightly as he entered their room.

Josh grunted without looking up from the book in his hands that he clearly wasn't reading. He crossed his legs and turned away.

"I'm going for a shower," George said. No response. He took a breath, thought better of saying anything further, went to the bathroom and showered.

Josh was still sitting in the same position when he came out a few minutes later, but he looked somewhat less furious. It was difficult to be angry and sad at the same time.

George put on a pair of shorts and sat next to him, gently lifting Josh's chin with his finger. "Don't be like this," he chided gently.

Josh sniffed and tried to smile.

"Please?"

"You thought he was attractive."

"Yeah. I did. Because he was."

"And he liked you."

"True."

Josh ducked his head, his hair flopping in front of his face.

"He liked you more, though," George said.

"Rubbish."

"No." George pulled the book away. "You should have seen the way he was looking at you. He thought you were gorgeous."

Josh lifted his head again but still wouldn't make eye contact.

"And I'd have to agree."

"You're just trying to make me feel better."

"I'm not. Well, I am trying to make you feel better, but it's the truth."

Josh didn't reply.

George stood up and went in search of a T-shirt. "I wish you could see yourself the way I see you."

Josh watched George quietly. For the past two days, he'd been trying to find the courage to make the offer. He knew it was worth more than the one he had made on their wedding night, and it was a far greater sacrifice.

George picked out a plain white T-shirt and had barely pulled it over his head when Josh got up and intercepted, putting his hands in the way to stop it from going any further.

"Keep it off," he said.

"Why?"

"Because I want to look at you."

George lifted the T-shirt away and examined Josh's face, trying to make sense of his unusual request.

"Sit with me?"

George did as he asked.

Josh sat, silent, thoughtful, inhaling deep, slow breaths, his hands spanning the smooth skin of George's bare arms, fingertips lingering on each wrist, his eyes closed as he focused on the sensation of the pulse. He lifted George's hand to kiss his palm and pressed it to his cheek.

All the while, George kept his gaze on Josh's face, confused, enthralled by his actions.

"You are so perfect," Josh said, the flats of his hands now against George's arms. He ran them up over his shoulders, his neck, his face. "So perfect." He looked into George's eyes and smiled. Then he started to cry, but there was no sorrow behind the tears. "I want to feel this perfect," he said. He brought his hands back down George's chest. It wasn't sexual, or even physical. It was emotional, psychological. "You can paint me."

George backed off slightly. He hadn't meant to.

"Or draw me. I want to see what you see, because I can't see past these." Josh lifted his sleeve-covered arms.

"Will you take off your shirt?" George asked.

Josh raised his arms higher. "Will you take it off for me?"

George shook his head. "No. You need to do it."

Josh stalled, uncertain, but then slowly started to unfasten the buttons. There were only two of them, and he had to pull the shirt over his head to take it off. He paused for a few seconds with his arms still inside the sleeves. But when he looked up at George, he saw only patience and understanding. Somehow, knowing he could stop if he wanted to gave him the courage to continue. He shook himself free and put the shirt to one side, instinctively crossing his arms. George smiled in encouragement, and Josh slowly relaxed, letting his hands fall to his lap.

"Why?" he asked.

"Why what?"

"Take off my shirt."

George paused, trying to word the reasons before he gave them.

"And don't tell me it's because you want to look, when you could've been looking at—"

"Stop it," George pleaded. Josh gasped in surprise. George softened. "I'm sorry. I didn't know how to tell him about you."

"You didn't want to tell him you were gay in case he wasn't."

"Yes. I don't want to look at anyone else, Josh." George placed his palm on Josh's chest and kept it there, concentrating on the gentle beat of his heart. Josh blushed. "I promise you, however good-looking that guy was, you won't catch me eating melon off his…pecs." George was nervous but trying not to show it, because Josh was nervous enough for the both of them.

"So, if I am going to draw or paint you, you're going to have to deal with being naked, or semi-naked at least."

Josh's eyes opened wide.

"Not that I'm planning on a nude here, although I don't want clothes getting in the way, and if I do this and then you can't cope with seeing it… I know it sounds a bit crazy and superstitious,

but I won't destroy or paint over what I create, because…
I just won't."

Josh shrugged. "OK. That makes sense, but do you have to
include my arms?"

"I guess not. I could do something, ooh, I don't know—maybe
a bit like the *Venus de Milo*?" George's eyes twinkled. Josh stuck
out his tongue. George grinned. "I still need to figure out the
pose. We can try some positions where your arms are hidden."

"Like what?"

"Hmm." George drummed on his chin while he thought.
"What about if you lie down with your hands behind your head?"

Josh slid down the bed and positioned himself accordingly.

"No. It makes you look…" George ran his fingers over Josh's
chest, tracing the dip from his ribcage into the hollow of his belly.

"Emaciated?" Josh suggested. George sensed he was starting
to feel more comfortable.

"No," he laughed, "although you're very slim. How's that
possible when you eat the junk you do?"

"You mean the junk I used to before somebody started force-
feeding me vegetables sautéed with tarragon and rosemary?"

"See? You're learning. That actually sounds quite nice.
Asparagus, spring onions, perhaps a couple of sweet red
peppers…" George refocused on the pose. "How about on your
side, leaning on your arm."

Josh duly obliged and allowed George to move his legs, pulling
his topmost knee up towards his groin, then pushing it straight
again. He positioned the open book by Josh's side and stepped
back. "No. Too unnatural."

"What about…" Josh moved and lay on his front, leaning on
his forearms, with the book between them.

George frowned. "Can't see your face, or much else of interest."
He took a moment to glance along Josh's back, following the
curve of his buttocks under the soft linen. It was a beautiful pose,
but it didn't bring out the features he wanted.

Josh sighed and sat up again. "You figure it out," he relented, reluctantly.

George examined his face. This had to be Josh's decision, and he couldn't force him nor even so much as try to persuade him to do this. Yet he realised Josh was desperate to give his consent and in need of some gentle reassurance and encouragement. George sat on the bed and took Josh's hands, kissing each finger, the way he always did. He paused, then slowly turned Josh's hands palms up, copying exactly what Josh had done to him.

"This is no different to my drawings," he said. He covered as many of the circular burns as he could with his fingertips. "Why should you be ashamed? You did it for me. This is a sketch of how you felt when you gave up on us. Not that I'm saying it's a good thing or the right thing to do. But what I see here—" he smoothed his palms over the criss-cross cuts "—is the life we could have had. Here—" he ran his fingertip back and forth over the lines "—we are dancing together through the night in an incredible club lit with strobes and neon. And here—" he traced two lines that formed an X like crossed swords "—we are on holiday. Somewhere amazing, like—"

"Ibiza," Josh interrupted. George looked up at his face. He was smiling. George started to laugh.

"If you like."

"And what about here?" Josh said, suddenly serious again. He held up his wrists. George wrapped his fingers around them.

"I'd die for you too," he whispered. He opened his eyes again. "Kiss me."

Josh shuffled forward and leaned close until their lips gently came together and remained in contact for many seconds.

They slowly pulled apart, never breaking eye contact. Josh had given his permission; now he was waiting for an answer.

"Yes," George said. "I will paint you. And then you will see."

From This Day

WHATCHA READING?"

"Mills and Boon," Josh answered without looking up from the open book. He had been lying on his front in the same position, save for turning pages or occasionally stretching his back, for the best part of three hours.

George lay down next to him and lifted the book off the blanket. He laughed in disbelief. "No way. It actually is Mills and Boon!"

"I'd read all the geeky books I brought with me."

"And where did you find that piece of trash?"

"In your suitcase."

"Just as well I didn't pack it, then."

"No. You must've sneaked it in later."

George pushed him, and Josh rolled onto his back, putting his hands up to shield his eyes, although the sun had descended low into the evening sky.

"I can't believe we're going home tomorrow," George said with a heavy sigh.

Josh turned to study his face. He did look sad to be leaving, and the feeling was mutual, not least because of how their behaviour and feelings for each other had transformed during the past few days. The changes, Josh knew, were not permanent, but it didn't matter; their love was.

"We should go back to the hotel," Josh suggested.

"Yeah." George sighed again. Josh poked him in the side, and he jumped.

"Don't get all melancholy."

"OK. I'll try not to."

"What've you been working on?" he asked, both as distraction and out of curiosity.

Before Josh had a chance to peek, George got up and closed his sketchbook. He would share when it was finished, but not before. Josh huffed but didn't push it further and instead lay on his back again, his eyes on the clear blue sky. George propped himself on one elbow and watched Josh's face.

"What?" Josh asked.

"Nothing."

Josh turned towards him, an eyebrow raised in query.

George fought a smile. "Just looking, that's all."

"OK."

"OK?"

"Yes. OK."

"You've changed your tune."

"I'm getting used to it." Josh's tone was flippant. "You've been staring at me all day."

"Not staring."

"If not staring…"

"Examining."

"Staring."

"I wasn't."

"You were too."

"Was not!"

"You w—"

George silenced him with his lips.

Josh snuggled closer, but then became quiet and still. "I need to tell you something," he said. "I should've told you months ago, but I didn't know how."

George waited.

"I kissed Ellie."

"Kissed, as in…?"

"Snogged."

George took a couple of breaths and said nothing.

"I'm sorry I didn't tell you."

"Why are you telling me now?"

"Because…we won't be here again, so there won't be a place to remind us of it."

George rolled away.

"I'm sorry," Josh repeated.

"It's OK."

"It's not."

"Yes, it is," George said earnestly.

Josh sat up and looked at him in confusion.

"It was around the time you built the snowman, wasn't it?"

"Yes."

"Which is why it's OK."

Josh frowned, not really understanding George's reaction. He'd expected him to be angry, hurt, or both.

"Sometimes you're gonna do crazy things," George said. "We both have to accept that, because it's part of you." He stood up and held out his hands to Josh. "And I love *all* of you."

Those words. How long he had waited to hear those words. To finally know that it was OK to be who he was; to be loved, unconditionally. Hearing them filled him with such happiness and relief, he could feel it rising up through his body, a transfusion erasing the scars, the sorrow, the years of loneliness. He took George's hands and looked up into his eyes, holding his gaze. George gently pulled him to his feet.

"Tell me again," Josh whispered.

"I love *all* of you, Joshua Sandison-Morley. Even if you are a bit mad in the head and have the longest name in the world."

As George leaned forward to kiss him, Blue pushed his way between their legs.

Josh laughed. "I think someone else needs your love too."

Blue wagged his tail, spraying them both with wet sand, and tore off in the direction of the hotel. A few seconds later, when he realised they weren't following, he came running back and nosed at George's hand.

"OK, we're coming now," he said. Blue darted off again, and George shook his head. "Must've been taking bossiness tips from Miranda."

"Miranda?"

"The Pomeranian."

"Who calls a dog Miranda?"

George picked up his sketchpad and slung the blanket over his shoulder. "Who calls a dog Blue?"

"Blue's a great name. Better than Miranda, that's for sure."

"You really don't like them, do you?"

"The sister wives? I don't dislike them, but they make me feel a little uneasy with their weird symbiosis."

"It can't be symbiosis. They're the same species."

"Remind me again which one of us is the geek."

"Um, both of us?"

Barefooted, hand in hand, they set off along the beach.

"So, was it any good?" George asked, after a few minutes of strolling in silence. Josh looked puzzled. "The Mills and Boon?"

"Oh!"

"You thought I meant kissing Ellie, didn't you?"

"Well, erm…"

George tutted. They continued walking. "So?"

"The Mills and Boon?"

"Yes, the Mills and Boon."

"You know, it was the usual sort of thing. Basically, there's this guy, a farmer, handsome, rugged, acts all tough."

"Typical Mills and Boon character."

"Hmm. And you'd know that how, exactly?"

"Educated guess." George blushed.

"Please tell me you've never read romance novels." George whistled quietly to himself. "Good grief." Josh laughed. "You never fail to amaze me."

"So this farmer, then?"

"Well, he meets the most unlikely person to have a relationship with—a bookish academic, a psychologist, I believe."

"Really? Sounds improbable."

"Yes. That's what I thought. And he's shattered."

"Who is?"

"The farmer. Because he thinks his love is unrequited, and really, behind the tough outer shell, he's quite sensitive and vulnerable. Kind of arty too. He paints and draws, and he's very talented. So, he runs away—goes off to live in America, on a ranch, would you believe?"

"That's seriously far-fetched."

"And, you know, he's lying to himself, pretending he doesn't care anymore, because he's still in love with the other guy. Meanwhile, the psychologist is also living a lie, acting as if he never loved him to begin with. But then, he gets a letter from the ranch, telling him that the farmer, who turns out to be the love of his life, has fallen for someone else."

"No way! What does he do?"

"He calls him up, but he still can't bring himself to admit that he loves him, although it is kind of obvious from the start if you read between the lines."

"What happens? Do they end up getting together?"

"Of course they do. It's a Mills and Boon!"

"I see."

"George!"

"Sorry." He grinned. "What was it really about?"

"No idea. I only read the first page."

They reached their room, and George stopped to fish the keycard out of his pocket. Josh wasn't paying any attention, so was taken somewhat by surprise when George pushed him up against the door.

"So," George said. Josh lifted his face until their lips were only an inch apart.

"So?" he repeated, inhaling George's breath. He heard the card slide through the lock and felt the door ease open behind him. George moved them both into the room, pushing the door shut with his foot. Josh allowed himself to be steered backwards until he fell onto the bed. George landed on top of him and gazed down at him. There was love there, and something else.

"I don't want to do it." George's tone was quiet yet assured.

"What do you mean? Paint me?"

"No. The other."

"Are you scared you'd hurt me?"

"Maybe, a little. I don't need to—*we* don't need to. I promised."

"What if I did it to you instead?"

George rolled away and sat on the edge of the bed, staring at his bare feet. "Does it matter this much to you?"

"No." Josh pulled himself to his knees and shuffled up behind George, tenderly kissing his cheek. "It really doesn't matter *this* much."

George took hold of his hands and squeezed. "We make love, don't we?" he asked. "What we've got—it's beyond sex. And what we did the other day—that was incredible. When I said I wanted to make love to you *my way*, that's what I was wishing for. To give you what you give me, but if it hadn't ever happened, or it never happens again, it wouldn't matter."

Josh sighed, trying to think how best to explain. "It was amazing, you're right. And we do make love, but—when I told Ellie I'd never kissed anyone before you, she was shocked, and I keep thinking—" He bit his lip nervously. "I really don't want to be a forty-year-old virgin."

George turned and looked at him, trying not to smile.

"It's not funny."

George laughed gently. "It is a bit. Still, that gives us eighteen months or so to work it out, and talk about it, because maybe you need to rethink this."

"Why?"

"What does it mean to lose your virginity? Penetration?"

"I guess."

"OK, and what about Elise and Lorna?"

"Who?"

"The sister wives."

"Oh, well, erm..." Josh frowned and thought for a while but couldn't come up with an answer or, at least, not one that supported his point of view. "I don't know," he admitted. "What does it mean?"

"It means giving yourself to another person, letting go. It's about trust."

Josh was confused. This was all new territory for him, and he needed time to work it out in his mind.

George squeezed his hand again to get his attention. "Look, much as I think it's the craziest reason, if it's important to you—" He became solemn once more. "It's just—it's a very long time since—"

"Sam?" Josh finished. He'd suspected it all along.

"Yeah, Sam." George hissed the name in anger. "To put it in the bluntest of terms, he liked to fuck me. And it hurt."

"In what way?"

"Only physically. It was only ever sex, and most of the time, I enjoyed what we were doing, which makes me sound like some kind of freak, but sometimes... Anyway, it was a long time ago."

"What about Joe?"

"Err, no."

"But you said you slept together."

"Slept as in shared a bed, and yes, we got physically close, but not that. The thing with Joe—I can see now he pushed me into it, and I went along with it because I knew it wouldn't last, and I never stopped hoping for us. But there's a whole load of other stuff going on there, to do with the ranch, and I think Joe's in love with Ray. Although Ray's straight and has been happily married since the age of eighteen. He and his wife were high school sweethearts."

Josh shuffled sideways and sat on the edge of the bed next to George. "Why have you never told me any of this?"

"It didn't come up. Plus, I only just figured it out—how Sam affected me, I mean. What you said, about visualising my feelings? You're right. I started thinking back over my relationships—

why I got involved, how they made me feel—and if I do it with colours and images, then it starts to make sense. Like me and Kris? That's a kind of red-and-green stripe, like a candy bar. It reminds me of that rhyme Adele used to chant at primary school."

Josh recited, "Red and green should never be seen, unless there's something in between."

"Yep. She was ever the designer!"

"So who's the 'in between'? Shaunna?"

"Maybe. Barley sugars."

"Barley sugars?"

George nodded. "Shaunna. When I think of her, I think of barley sugar sweets."

"Yes, I can see why you would."

"Those twisty orange sticks we used to buy? I hated them when we were little, but when I was in America, I really missed them. I got terrible cravings."

"She missed you too," Josh said.

George smiled and became thoughtful once more. "Then there's Jono, who is just like the sunshine—so bright and warm and yellow."

"And big," Josh pointed out.

George laughed. "That as well."

"He made you happy, didn't he?"

"Yeah. He did. We needed each other, with his mum's drug addiction and, well, I guess my mum's bingo addiction. She was a mess after Dad left."

George smiled apologetically, but Josh simply nodded, giving him permission to keep talking.

"I still hate him for it. My dad. Don't get me wrong—she's always been mouthy and smoked too much. And worn those stupid rollers. But when she was younger, she was so beautiful. I still think she is, of course, but I mean in a stereotypical way, with her big blonde hair, like the most stunning white lily in bloom, all perfume and petals. And she wore the nicest clothes and high heels."

He closed his eyes and described what he saw. "She'd wander around the house, cigarette hanging from her mouth, pulling out her rollers with one hand and zipping her skirt with the other, shoving her feet into her stilettos on the move, shouting, 'Georgie? Where the hell are yer, lad? Gonna be late a-bloody-gain at this rate.'" He opened his eyes again, and they sparkled with joy. "Every single morning, the same thing."

Josh was listening and smiling. Yes, George had always talked a lot, but it was the inconsequential things, like what to have for breakfast, the adventures of the Dog People he met in the woods or some wild animal that he'd seen on his way home from work. It was hardly ever about how he was feeling because he could only get so far before that mental lock clicked shut and the words wouldn't come. Now, it seemed that between them, they'd found the key, and all his feelings could escape. Alas, it wasn't all sunshine and flowers.

"Sam is..." George shook his head vigorously, like he was trying to shake the thoughts out. "He's like a dank, dark winter's day. Not even colour. Just this grey, cold, awful..." He screwed his eyes tight shut against the memory.

Josh gently took his hand. "You don't have to tell me."

"I know." George fell silent for a while, taking deep breaths and stroking the back of Josh's hand with his thumb. "What I was gonna say is, Sam and Joe don't mean much to me. I was an idiot for not realising they were using me, but I don't really feel anything for them. So, Sam's grey and Joe's kind of beige and dusty, like the tracks around the ranch. Except when I think about the way he was with Ray, and then it starts to look a bit like the Yellow Brick Road. I do kinda feel sorry for him, though, because I've been there."

"We both have."

"True. And he kept it well hidden."

"Weird."

"Uh-huh. Family trait."

"Falling in love with people you can't have?"

"Actually…" George pushed Josh back onto the bed and straddled him. "I meant not saying how we feel."

Josh pretended to struggle. "And what colour am I?"

"You make me sound like Alice."

"Do you see colours when you experience emotions?"

"No. It's like you said—if I can visualise it, I can say it."

"Then it's not synaesthesia."

"Could it be related?"

"Possibly. I've no idea."

"But you're a bookish academic psychologist. Or a geek, as us tough, rugged farmer types like to call them."

"I still don't know everything."

"Oh, really?" George tormented.

"Really." Josh laughed, once again wriggling in a feigned attempt to break free. George had him pinned down by the arms and was kissing his neck, his intentions very clear.

"Is this OK?" he asked.

"Depends." Josh shivered, his body starting to tingle in that unfamiliar way.

"On what?"

"If you're going to tell me how you feel."

"I want to make love to you."

"What is the colour of this love?"

"All of them."

"Like the brownish-grey you get when you rinse your paintbrushes?"

"Like the rainbow." George began to unbutton Josh's shirt, his hands trembling as he tried to push away the memory of the last time he had done it.

Josh steadied George's hands with his own. "We'll do it together," he said.

Whether shaking, numb-fingered or fully functioning, unbuttoning a shirt with four hands was no easy feat, and their joint failure was the perfect tonic, soon quelling any residual distress. A couple of minutes on, they were giggling helplessly, and half of the buttons were still fastened.

George flopped onto the bed alongside Josh. "See, this is what making love is about." He rolled onto his side and put an arm behind his head.

Josh shuffled up and sat cross-legged, his part-undone shirt falling open, with no attempt to cover himself up. Indeed, he didn't even seem to be aware of the fact that his bare shoulder and chest were on display.

"We kind of lost the moment there, didn't we?" he said, and continued to speak, for what it was worth.

George had stopped listening, although his eyes were fully taking in every aspect of Josh and of his current pose: bare feet under knees draped in loose linen, light blue turned lilac by the peach-red of the setting sun; one slender, milky hand resting in his lap, the other slung carelessly behind his head, the crumpled sleeve exposing his forearm; the V of his open white shirt showing off his smooth, pale chest, shoulder, neck and chin; his white-blonde, sun-bleached hair; the animated blue sparkling of his eyes; the blush-pink of his lips—George suddenly realised they were moving. Josh was still talking. George met his gaze, diving deep into it.

"What did you say?" he asked breathlessly.

"I said we lost the moment, although…I think I might have been wrong."

"I got that bit. What did you say after that?"

"I said it's going dark."

"Oh."

"And also—" Josh slid down the bed so they were face-to-face "—I asked if you'd like a lick of my lollipop."

"Are you being rude?"

"No." Josh put his hand under the pillow. "I meant an actual lollipop." He held up the two sweets.

George laughed and took one, and they lay, side by side, with their lollipops in their mouths, the only sound the occasional clack of hard-boiled sugar against teeth.

George spoke around the obstruction. "You know how people always ask what you did on holiday?"

"Mmm?"

"Do you think they do it when you get back from honeymoon?"

"I doubt it. Why?"

"Just wondering what we're gonna tell them if they do."

"We can tell them we ate lots of fruit."

George's eyebrows rose.

"From the most exquisite dining table."

"You're really gonna say that?"

"And that we watched a beautiful sunset whilst sucking lollipops."

"They'll think it's a euphemism."

"Maybe it will be."

"Or we could just tell them we spent the whole time making love."

"Now, is that your way or my way?"

"*Our* way."

The best way.

And the glorious fiery ball of the spent midsummer sun fell silently into the sea.

Crunch.

"You still didn't answer my question."

"Didn't you just—"

THE END

About the Author

Debbie McGowan is an author and publisher based in a semi-rural corner of Lancashire, England. She writes character-driven, realist fiction, celebrating life, love and relationships. A working-class girl, she 'ran away' to London at seventeen, was homeless, unemployed and then homeless again, interspersed with animal rights activism (all legal, honest ;)) and volunteer work as a mental health advocate. At twenty-five, she went back to college to study social science—tough with two toddlers, but they had a 'stay at home' dad, so it worked itself out. These days, the toddlers are young women (much to their chagrin) and Debbie teaches undergraduate students, writes novels and runs an independent publishing company, occasionally grabbing an hour's sleep where she can.

Social Media Links

Website: debbiemcgowan.co.uk and hidingbehindthecouch.com
Newsletter Signup: eepurl.com/b8emHL
Blog: deb248211.blogspot.com
Facebook: facebook.com/DebbieMcGowanAuthor and facebook.com/beatentrackpublishing
Twitter: @writerdebmcg
YouTube: youtube.com/deb248211
Instagram: instagram/writerdebmcg
Tumblr: writerdebmcg.tumblr.com
LinkedIn: uk.linkedin.com/in/writerdebmcg
Goodreads: goodreads.com/DebbieMcGowan
Books2Read: https://books2read.com/DebbieMcGowan

By the Author

I'm not a single-genre author, for which I make no apology. Nor do I write stories of a specific length; I believe a story should be as long as it needs to be.

Thus, to assist you in navigating my catalogue, I've also included the closest-fitting genres and types of publication.

Hiding Behind The Couch Series
(Contemporary/Literary Fiction)
The ongoing story of 'The Circle'...
Nine friends from high school;
Nine friends for life.

The Story So Far...
(in chronological order)

- *Beginnings* (Novella)
- *Ruminations* (Novel)
- *Class-A* (Short Story – also in *Take a Chance* anthology)
- *Hiding Behind The Couch* (Season One)
- *No Time Like The Present* (Season Two)
- *The Harder They Fall* (Season Three)
- *Crying in the Rain* (Novel)
- *First Christmas* (Novella)
- *In The Stars Part I: Capricorn–Gemini* (Season Four)
- **Breaking Waves (Novella)**
- *Chain of Secrets* (Novella – also in *Love Unlocked* anthology)
- *In The Stars Part II: Cancer–Sagittarius* (Season Five)

- *A Midnight Clear* (Novella – also in *Boughs of Evergreen* anthology)
- *Red Hot Christmas* (Novella)
- *Two By Two* (Season Six)
- *Hiding Out* (Novella – CHO Crossover)
- *Those Jeffries Boys* (Novel)
- *The WAG and The Scoundrel* (Gray Fisher #1)
- *Perfect Tenor* (Novella)
- *The Lost Mitten* (see 'Children's Stories')
- *Reunions* (Season Seven)
- *Tabula Rasa* (Gray Fisher #2)
- *Breakfast at Cordelia's Aquarium* (Short Story)
- *Reverberations* (Novel)
- *To Be Sure* (Novella – also in *Never Too Late* anthology)
- *What A Scorcher!* (Flash Fiction)
- *Goth of Christmas Past* (Front of House #1)
- *The Advent of Reason* (Novella)
- ***Not My Christmas* (Novella)**
- *Highlights* ~ co-written with A.M. Leibowitz (Short Story – Notes from Boston meets Hiding Behind The Couch)
- *Distractions* (Gray Fisher #3)

Checking Him Out Series
(M/M and LGBTQ Romance)

- *Checking Him Out* (Book One)
- *Checking Him Out For the Holidays* (Novella)
- *Hiding Out* (Novella – Noah and Matty – HBTC Crossover)
- *Taking Him On* (Book Two – Noah and Matty)
- *Checking In* (Book Three)
- *The Making of Us* (Book Four – Jesse and Leigh)

Seeds of Tyrone Series
(M/M Romance)
~ co-written with Raine O'Tierney

- *Leaving Flowers* (Book One)
- *Where the Grass is Greener* (Book Two)
- *Christmas Craic and Mistletoe* (Book Three)

Stand-Alone Stories

- *Champagne* (LGBTQ Historical Novel)
- 'Time to Go' (Contemporary Short in *Story Salon Big Book of Stories*)
- *And The Walls Came Tumbling Down* (Sci-fi Novel)
- *No Dice* (Sci-fi Novel)
- *Double Six* (Sci-fi Novel)
- *Sugar and Sawdust* (M/M Romance Short Story)
- *Cherry Pop Valentine* (M/M Romance Short Story)
- *Coming Up* ~ co-written with Al Stewart (LGBTQ Short Story)
- *Of the Bauble* (LGBTQ Fantasy Romance Novella)
- *So Long, Little Black Diamonds* (True Short Story)
- *The Pastor's Last Drop* (Ongoing Historical Novel – Wattpad)
- *When Skies Have Fallen* (LGBTQ Historical Romance Novel)
- *A Snowy Ball* (When Skies Have Fallen Novelette)
- *The Great Village Bun Fight* (LGBTQ Comedy Novella – also in *Seasons of Love* anthology)
- 'Oh No She Didn't!' (LGBTQ Short Story in *Upstaged!: an anthology of women who love women in the performing arts*)
- *The Great Pretendo* (Flash Fiction)
- 'Nina, Pretty Ballerina' (Short Story in *Play On…: a collection of short stories, poetry and prose, inspired by the songs of ABBA*)
- *Meredith's Dagger* (Contemporary/Historical Feminist/LGBTQ Novel)

Audiobooks

- *And The Walls Came Tumbling Down* – Narrated by Hannibal Mills
- *Checking Him Out* – Narrated by Tim Larkfield
- *Of The Bauble* – Narrated by Jack Hardman
- *The Great Village Bun Fight* – Narrated by Jack Hardman
- *When Skies Have Fallen* – Narrated by Tim Holbourne

Children's Stories (written as J.S. Morley)

- *The Lost Mitten* ~ illustrated by Sofia Oxelstrand
- *Chompy the Velociraptor* ~ illustrated by Kate Andrew
- *Zoom the Pterodactyl*

www.hidingbehindthecouch.com
www.debbiemcgowan.co.uk
www.beatentrackpublishing.com/debbiemcgowan

Beaten Track Publishing

For more titles from Beaten Track Publishing,
please visit our website:

https://www.beatentrackpublishing.com

Thanks for reading!